Voices *from the* Mist

Also by Bea Carlton
in Large Print:

In the House of the Enemy
Moonshell

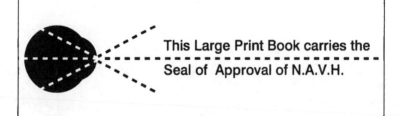

Voices *from the* Mist

Bea Carlton

Thorndike Press • Waterville, Maine

Sequel to Deadly Gypsy Blue.

Published in 2003 by arrangement with Bea Carlton.

Thorndike Press® Large Print Christian Mystery Series.

The tree indicium is a trademark of Thorndike Press.

The text of this Large Print edition is unabridged.
Other aspects of the book may vary from the original edition.

Set in 16 pt. Plantin by Al Chase.

Printed in the United States on permanent paper.

Library of Congress Cataloging-in-Publication Data

Carlton, Bea.
    Voices from the mist / by Bea Carlton.
        p. cm.
    ISBN 0-7862-5317-7 (lg. print : hc : alk. paper)
    1. Stalking victims — Fiction.   2. New Mexico — Fiction.
    3. Large type books.   I. Title.
    PS3553.A736V65 2003
    813'.54—dc21   2003047373

Dedicated lovingly to Lee Mowery,
who is everything a big sister should be:
thoughtful, supportive and caring.

As the Founder/CEO of NAVH, the only national health agency solely devoted to those who, although not totally blind, have an eye disease which could lead to serious visual impairment, I am pleased to recognize Thorndike Press as one of the leading publishers in the large print field.

Founded in 1954 in San Francisco to prepare large print textbooks for partially seeing children, NAVH became the pioneer and standard setting agency in the preparation of large type.

Today, those publishers who meet our standards carry the prestigious "Seal of Approval" indicating high quality large print. We are delighted that Thorndike Press is one of the publishers whose titles meet these standards. We are also pleased to recognize the significant contribution Thorndike Press is making in this important and growing field.

Lorraine H. Marchi, L.H.D.
Founder/CEO
NAVH

Chapter 1

Adria Graham lifted beseeching gray-blue eyes to her cousin Kandy Graham's face. "I know it sounds like I'm being paranoid but I'm not. Believe me, Kandy, I'm not! That creepy man is following me everywhere I go!"

Kandy frowned, her deep blue eyes narrowing as she stared at her cousin, who at twenty-five was six months younger than Kandy. "But why would a man follow you around Albuquerque when he isn't anyone you even know?"

"I don't know," Adria said despondently. "Maybe he read one of my newspaper articles and got some kind of fixation about me. Who knows? In this crazy world of weirdoes, do they need a reason to do anything?"

The shriek of a police siren in the distance came dully to their ears above the subdued sound of the busy city street outside.

"Adria, I think you're working too hard. Maybe you need a rest. Take some time off — you deserve it after this last series of investigative articles you did. Come up to The Lodge with me, sleep late, tramp in the woods and relax."

"You think I'm imagining things," Adria said reproachfully. "That's what my boss said too. Okay! Maybe I will take off a few days. But I'm not imagining that creep following me!"

"When did you first notice this man?" Kandy asked.

Adria jumped up and paced the floor in agitation. Both young women were dressed for bed. Kandy had caught the bus down from Taos, New Mexico to spend the weekend with Adria in Albuquerque. "About two months ago," Adria replied. "I was in the old part of Albuquerque and it was getting dark. After interviewing a woman in a cafe, I started out the door. Four men were lounging around a car parked at the curb, passing around a bottle."

"You are going to get yourself in deep trouble or killed traipsing around this city by yourself at all hours," Kandy warned.

"It's part of my job," Adria said impatiently. "Anyway, when I stepped out onto the sidewalk one of the men yelled at me, using obscenities."

"What did he say?"

"He used my name and yelled something about females meddling with men's work and it could get me killed — or worse. I

8

knew he was referring to an article I had done recently on the 'coyotes' who smuggle illegals across the Mexican border. In the article I stressed the dangers to their victims.

"I turned around and tried to get back into the cafe but instantly the four were all around me, laughing and making insulting remarks. They reeked of alcohol. I have never been more frightened in my life!"

Adria took a deep breath and Kandy said breathlessly, "What happened?"

"That's when I first saw that man," Adria said. "One minute he wasn't there and the next he was. He didn't say a word but just started clearing the men from around me. He was tall and thin as a whip but he could use his arms and feet and knees like a judo expert. He tumbled one man into the street, another against the side of the building and the third he picked up and literally hurled down the sidewalk. The fourth took to his heels like the devil was after him."

"You mean this man rescued you and you call him a weirdo?"

"Not then, of course. I tried to thank him but he only gave me a queer little salute and waved me to my car. A couple of the men were getting up so I jumped in my car and took off."

"And you've been seeing him around ever since?"

"Yes, I interview people and do research all over Albuquerque and nearly always I see him somewhere before I get home. Sometimes only a glimpse of him but there is no mistaking his tall, skinny physique."

"What's wrong with having a man around to protect you from harm?" Kandy asked with a giggle.

"It's creepy, that's what! Besides, how do I know I don't need a protector from him?"

"Have you ever talked to your champion and asked him why he's following you?"

"I've tried to talk to him but he does a disappearing act as soon as he realizes I've seen him."

"Is this admirer good-looking?" Kandy asked mischievously from the middle of the bed, hugging her pajama-clad knees to her chest with slim arms. Her dark eyes danced.

"It isn't funny," Adria said sharply. She slumped down on the edge of the bed and said soberly, "I really don't know what he looks like. He wears an old slouch hat pulled down on his head. The one time I was close to him — at the cafe — I sensed he was rather young. But with the hat on and a bristly three or four day stubble covering his face I really couldn't say what he looked like."

"Maybe he's someone you know."

"No, I may not be able to see his face very well but I would know his almost emaciated, thin build if I had ever seen it before."

"That's strange that he follows you around and yet won't talk to you or let you see his face well."

"Tell me about it!"

"How does he dress?"

"Nondescript. Blue jeans, an old Levi jacket, athletic shoes — all worn but clean looking. His hair is longish, curly and brown, I think. I especially remember his hands: thin, long fingers and very strong. I shiver when I recall how he tossed those young men around like rag dolls."

"Well, he has never harmed you so why don't you just forget about him."

"How can I forget about him when he's the last thing I see before I go to bed at night!"

"What?"

"It's ten-thirty and about my bedtime," Adria said mysteriously. She motioned, "Turn off that lamp and I'll turn off the main light." Mystified, Kandy obeyed. The room was now only dimly lit by the streetlight outside.

"Now, come over here," Adria said, moving to the drapery covered window.

When Kandy joined her, Adria pushed the curtain aside slightly and peered out. "There's my champion," she said, sarcastically.

Kandy put her face next to Adria's and stared out onto the street below.

Standing across the street, at the edge of the light shed by a lone streetlight, was the form of a tall, thin male. His shadowy form was not distinct but his head was tilted back as if he was gazing at the window where they stood.

"He must have seen the drape move," Adria said softly as the form abruptly swung about and moved away rapidly into the darkness. "He usually stands there like that for several minutes, just staring up at my window. He even knows which room I sleep in! Now, do you think I'm imagining things?"

"How long has he been seeing you to bed at night?" Kandy asked gravely. "And yes, I agree this isn't your imagination and it is creepy!"

"I first noticed him down there a couple of weeks ago," Adria said with a shudder. "But I have no idea how long he's been doing that."

"I think it's time you got out of town for a while," Kandy said, her dark eyes serious.

"How about taking that leave of absence and going home with me to The Lodge for a couple of weeks? That would give your admirer time to forget about you, and you a chance to rest up."

"I'll do it," Adria decided suddenly. "That kook couldn't possibly find me up in the woods near Taos."

Chapter 2

Adria swung her small red Honda onto Highway 68, the last leg of their trip to Taos. She glanced over at her cousin, sleeping peacefully on the laid-back seat.

"Hey, sleepy head, wake up." Adria's voice sounded loud above the soft purr of the car engine.

Kandy stretched her arms above her head and sleepily opened her eyes. "Whad'ja wake me up for?" she said around a leisurely yawn.

"Because I'm getting sleepy and I need someone to talk to," Adria said.

"Sorry to conk out on you as soon as we got out of Albuquerque," Kandy said, "but staying up till midnight packing and then getting up at five is a bummer. I was dead! But I'm much better now. Do you want me to drive?"

"No, I'm doing fine, if you'll just talk to me a little."

"Okay," Kandy said, "I'll ask the question I've been dying to ask. Are you serious about a guy yet?"

Adria cast a quick glance at her cousin and grimaced, "I wish I could say I was but I may be slated to be a bachelorette."

Kandy's dark eyes flashed, "Adria, you aren't still mooning over Giles, I hope!"

For a long moment Adria was silent, then she said morosely, "I wouldn't say I'm mooning over him. In fact I'm still furious with him for dumping me."

"But you haven't found anyone who comes up to him. That's it, isn't it?"

For several minutes Adria concentrated on her driving. When she finally spoke her voice was so low that Kandy could scarcely make out the words, "I guess I'm still puzzled. Giles and I had such a special relationship. I'm sure he felt the same way I did. Then just out of the blue, he writes that cold little note ending it. No explanation, just that it would never work."

"We never want to believe it could happen to us," Kandy said gently, "but maybe he found someone else down there in South America."

"Maybe," Adria said, "but if so, why didn't he just say so? I would have been deeply hurt but I could at least have gotten on with my life. But I keep feeling like it's an unfinished chapter. For one thing, I sent back the engagement ring he gave me, but he didn't send me back my high school class ring that he always wore around his neck."

"Maybe he lost it."

"Perhaps so, but that note just didn't sound like the Giles I went to college with. The man who told me the deepest secrets of his heart!"

"So you think he may come back yet," Kandy said softly.

"I-I don't know. I guess after almost two years that would be pretty foolish. But I just can't seem to get him out of my mind — or my heart."

"Did you write him after the note?"

"Yes, I'm ashamed to admit it, but I wrote him several letters. They didn't come back so I know he received them but he never wrote again."

Suddenly Adria straightened her shoulders. "I tell myself over and over what a fool I am but I can't seem to get over Giles Hughlet. I even dream about him sometimes. Sometimes he's calling me, begging me to help him." She turned misty eyes to Kandy, "Could that be God telling me that Giles needs me?"

"More likely it's your subconscious mind reflecting your refusal to accept the truth," Kandy said candidly. "Adria, you must forget that man! Get rough with yourself and make yourself believe that Giles Hughlet isn't coming back to you! Be as cruel to yourself as I'm being!"

For a long while Adria drove silently. Finally, a short way from Taos she pulled over and said abruptly, "I think you better drive the rest of the way. I'm getting a little rumdum."

Kandy took her place in the driver's seat and when they were en route again she looked anxiously at Adria. "I've upset you, haven't I? Talking about Giles, I mean, and advising you to forget him."

She laid her hand over Adria's hand lying on the seat and squeezed. "I'm sorry, Adria, I didn't mean to hurt you. I just want you to get on with your life. Remember," she finished teasingly, "you always said you wanted a husband and a whole houseful of kids."

"It's all right," Adria said gravely. "But I'm not sure I will ever get over Giles. Maybe I'm just a one man girl. Sometimes I have even thought it would be better for me if Giles had died. Then I would know what happened to him. Isn't that selfish?" she finished with a choked voice.

Kandy kept her full attention on her driving now as they wound through the narrow, crowded streets of Taos. Twice she had to come to a full stop as pedestrians moved across in front of the car. When she

17

spoke she changed the subject. "This place gets more crowded all the time. Even at eight-thirty in the morning it's crowded! I'm glad we live out in the forest and away from the tourists and traffic."

"I've always thought Taos was a fascinating place," Adria said, glad that they were again on a neutral subject. "I still like all the little shops tucked here and there. And the many cultures represented here always draw me to Taos. I never grow tired of it. I would live here if there was anything for me to make a living at."

"Train to be a forest ranger like me," Kandy said lightly.

"That suits you too," Adria said. "You always were a tomboy who liked the outdoors better than indoors. By the way, how is Sarge?"

"He's getting so smart that I sometimes forget he's a dog." Kandy chuckled, "That German Shepherd certainly doesn't think he's a dog! Remember, Giles even said that once."

"I know," Adria said. "Giles really loved that dog of yours. And next to you, I think Sarge liked him best. Even better than me — the old traitor!"

"Giles had a way with animals," Kandy said. "All dogs liked him. He should have been a veterinarian."

"I suppose," Adria said. Her throat was beginning to tighten and her heart was hammering. It was infuriating how talking or thinking about Giles affected her so strongly, even after almost two years of rejection! She pushed aside unwelcome thoughts of him and groped for something to change the subject.

"I'm sorry you couldn't bring Sarge with you. My landlady won't allow a pet of any kind, not even for a visit."

"That's all right," Kandy said. "He's at the veterinary clinic right now. He had a small tumor removed from his neck — nothing serious. I sure miss him."

Her expressive face suddenly showed pain as she glanced at Adria. "I take him everywhere with me now, even on the job. My superiors don't mind. You know, since that — that attack."

Kandy was now guiding the Honda expertly up a curving road, east out of town, climbing slowly toward the Carson National Forest.

"Does that assault still bother you?"

"Not often," Kandy said, "but once in a while something triggers the memory. Then I can still see that wild-eyed hoodlum coming for me and feel the terror I felt as he

19

began to pound me with his rock-hard fists."

"God surely must have been watching out for you," Adria said, "or you wouldn't be alive to tell it. They never did catch the man?"

"No, and I think that is what bothers me most. He's still out there and will probably do it again to someone." She turned wide eyes to Adria, "There was no motive that I — or the police — could reason out. He didn't take my money or even the forest service jeep I was driving."

"I know," Adria said softly. "But you said his eyes were kinda crazy-looking, so he must have been hopped up on something." Suddenly she shivered. "We both seem a little morbid today, so let's talk about something pleasant."

"Yes, let's!" Kandy agreed. "How about singing me a song. I haven't heard you sing in ages."

"Oh, please," Adria protested, "I haven't sung anything in a coon's age. I — say, there's a man ahead trying to wave us down. See? The hood to his car is up, so he must be having car trouble. Shouldn't we stop?"

Adria saw Kandy's face go as white as death, "No — no! That's something I never do anymore. That's the trick that man pulled to get me to stop two years ago, and he beat me nearly to death!" She had stepped on the gas and they were now past the man whose car was parked on the opposite side of the road.

"He doesn't look dangerous," Adria said. "He's driving a Lincoln Continental and his suit looks expensive, like a prosperous business man. I kinda hate to not offer help."

She had turned her head to look back at the stranded motorist they were rapidly leaving behind. "Besides, I've got some mace in the glove compartment. Couldn't the two of us handle him if he tried something?"

Kandy slowed the car somewhat but Adria could see the anguish on her pale face, so spoke quickly and decisively, "It might not be safe after all."

But Kandy slowed the car and gradually pulled over to the side of the road and stopped. She sat still for a moment and then grinned a lopsided, self-conscious smile. "Get your mace out. If he makes the slightest wrong move, we'll lower the boom on him."

"Are you sure we should," Adria said. Kandy's fear had caused unease to rise in her also.

"I wouldn't stop if you weren't along,

even with Sarge with me," Kandy said. "Let's drive back and only let the glass down enough to ask him who we should call to get him some help. We won't take him anywhere. Okay?"

"Agreed," Adria said as she opened the glove compartment and took out the small can of mace. As Kandy headed back, Adria laid her right hand containing the mace in her lap and drew a scarf over it.

Chapter 3

The stranger who stood by the brown and tan Lincoln Continental was at least six feet tall and perhaps twenty-eight or thirty. His expensive-cut suit covered broad, powerful shoulders and an athletic build. Sandy hair, receding from a high, strong forehead, glinted in the bright sunlight. A grin touched the wide, full lips as Adria's car slid to a stop near him.

He stepped to their car as Kandy rolled the car-window down about three inches. "My car seems to have left me stranded," he said pleasantly. "Would it be possible to get a lift to that little service station I passed a few miles back? I need to call a garage."

"We'll make the call for you," Kandy said. "Do you have a choice or shall we just send out anyone we can get."

"Just anyone will do," the stranger said. "I really don't know anyone in Taos except Larry Graham."

"Larry Graham?" Kandy asked cautiously. "You know him?"

"I don't actually know Larry," the man said. "But I'm going to if I can get to Taos. I've spoken to him on the phone a number of times. Do you know Larry Graham?"

Ignoring the question, Kandy asked abruptly, "What is your name?"

"I'm sorry, I should have introduced myself before," the man apologized. "I'm Gentry Howard of Bisbee, Arizona. I'm the manager of Gypsy Blue Enterprises, and I have some business to transact with Larry."

Suddenly Kandy rolled the window down and held out her hand. Her tense face relaxed and a grin appeared. "I'm Kandy Graham and I'm Larry's sister. Larry said you were coming in but he didn't expect you until tomorrow."

The big man's hazel green eyes lit up, "Say this is great! I'm glad to meet you, Kandy. Larry has mentioned you. I believe you're a forest ranger."

"Gentry, this is my cousin Adria Graham, from Albuquerque."

Gentry acknowledged the introduction courteously then said, "I know I arrived a day early but if Larry isn't around I can see some of the sights in the Taos area. I've never had a chance to sightsee here before."

"Taos is a fascinating place," Adria said.

"If I can get my car fixed, I aim to see it," Gentry said.

"The Lodge, where Larry and I live, isn't far," Kandy explained. "We have a handy man who can probably get your car going for you. If not, you can call a garage from there. And you're welcome to stay with us until you get it going."

"Say, that's nice of you, but I don't want to be a lot of bother," Gentry said quickly.

"It won't be any bother," Kandy assured him.

Gentry locked his car and folded his large frame into the back seat of the little Honda.

Gentry drew in his breath appreciatively. "This pine-scented air almost makes me intoxicated but I guess you girls are used to it."

"I never take this for granted," Kandy said softly as she swung the car off the highway onto a narrow graveled road which climbed steeply though a park-like grove of pines before it curved sharply and plunged into deep forest.

"I spent a great deal of time at The Lodge as I was growing up," Adria said, "and I'm like Kandy, I marvel every time I come back at the beauty of the forest. Ever changing, ever awe inspiring."

The car was now running smoothly along a ridge. Very near the right of the road, the mountain dropped away into a deep valley where glimpses of silver revealed a ribbon of water. Aspens stood out in pale-green splendor against the dark green of pine and fir and the silver of spruce. Bright scarlet, yellow, white, blue, violet and orange wild flowers spangled every patch of grass where the sun's rays reached.

A short while later, the car swung into a narrow lane which led to a clearing. A very large, two storied building built of peeled logs dominated the scene. A wide porch wound completely around the building. It was built on the slope of a hill, and towering pines stood like guarding sentinels about the grounds.

"That's The Lodge," Kandy said. "My ancestral abode."

"It certainly fits into the scenery," Gentry said. "I always wanted to live in a log house. However, this is more like a hotel it's so big. It's a beautiful place."

"Thanks," Kandy said, her white teeth flashed in a quick smile against dark tanned skin, before turning back to her driving. "I like it too."

They rattled across a log bridge which spanned a clear sparkling river, silver and green reflecting the trees which crowded its narrow sandy banks.

Parking beneath a magnificent old pine tree, Kandy got out and unlocked the back. Gentry quickly moved to take the two suitcases and overnight cases she was lifting out. Adria and Kandy led him down a path built of gray stone to a wide back door.

"We'll leave the suitcases here and go look for Fritz," Kandy said.

Fritz, a shriveled, slightly stooped old man, was quickly located in a workshop not far from the house. Kandy introduced him to Gentry and explained what was needed. As the handyman gathered up some tools, Kandy said softly to Gentry, "Fritz doesn't look like much but he's a genius with engines. He keeps our tractor, pick-up and cars in perfect shape."

"I appreciate the loan of him so much," Gentry said earnestly. "Except for changing a tire, I'm at a complete loss when anything goes wrong with my car."

"Larry plans for you to stay with us while you are here, so feel free to come on back here when your car is fixed. Fritz will drive you into Taos in our pick-up if he needs any parts."

"Say, that is sure decent of you all but I don't like to impose on you," Gentry protested.

Kandy held up a commanding brown hand, "Larry already had our housekeeper get you a room ready. So he'll be insulted if you don't stay here at The Lodge."

"Say no more, it will be my pleasure," Gentry said with a wide grin.

Fritz had now climbed behind the wheel of the pick-up, after loading his tool-box into the back. Gentry got in beside him and they drove away.

"Nice man," Adria commented as she and Kandy walked back toward the house. "And I think he likes you," she teased.

"Ha! Fat chance I'd have with any man with my cute cousin around," Kandy said lightly. "Besides, I'm committed to the life of a forest ranger."

"Forest rangers get married," Adria said seriously.

"Not this one," Kandy grimaced. "I never did see a man I liked as well as my dog Sarge. He's faithful, he adores me and it doesn't mean a thing to him that I'm plain and dark and skinny as a bean pole."

"You don't give a man a chance," Adria challenged.

"Who are you to talk," Kandy said. "Since you met Giles you have never seriously looked at another man. And he's been gone for almost two years."

Adria sighed, "I know, I guess the two of us are destined to be bachelorettes."

"Good for us!" Kandy said lightly. "At least we don't have to make a living for some no-good husband and don't stay home at night crying our eyes out because a loutish husband is out with another woman!"

"Wow! You've got it bad!" Adria laughed.

A sudden wicked gleam appeared in Kandy's dark eyes, "Of course when you find out who your secret admirer is, I may lose you from our old maid club!"

The fun went out of Adria's eyes as she lifted her heart-shaped face and stared out across the smooth expanse of lawn. "I-I'm afraid of him, Kandy. Why is he following me around like that? I can't forget the strength in his hands as he tossed those men about as if they were match sticks."

She turned tragic gray eyes to Kandy, "I'm almost afraid to go home anymore. If he decides to come out of the shadows some night, what would he do to me?"

Chapter 4

As Kandy and Adria entered the back entrance hall, steps were heard, then a slightly plump figure encased in a large coverall apron appeared. Perspiration stood out on the smooth pink forehead and a streak of flour ran across one round cheek. "Oh, it's you, Kandy. I couldn't imagine who it was. I thought you were going to stay the whole weekend with. . . ." Her china-blue eyes caught sight of Adria.

"Adria — do come in! So you two decided to come back here. Good! I've got some fresh-perked coffee and some cinnamon rolls just out of the oven."

Darting forward, she placed a quick peck on Adria's cheek. Like a plump little bird, she flitted back to the door and turned to survey the two girls reproachfully. "I do declare, you skinny girls! Not an ounce of fat on either of you! Come right into this kitchen and have some of my hot rolls."

As she preceded them into the sun-filled room beyond, Adria and Kandy exchanged amused looks. For as long as both could recall Kandy's older half-sister Sibyl, had been trying to fatten them up.

Sibyl was Benjamin Graham's only child by his first wife who had died when Sibyl was only five years old. Kandy's mother Katherine, Benjamin's second wife, was ill most of Kandy's life, before she died two years before. So the running of the Graham household had fallen early on Sibyl's capable shoulders, although she was only fifteen years older than Kandy.

Sibyl not only kept the Graham household going but had also mothered Larry and Kandy.

Adria felt a surge of pity for Sibyl. Now she had the added burden of the care of their District Attorney father. A few months before, Benjamin had suffered a debilitating stroke and was partially paralyzed. Refusing to stay in a nursing home, he had returned home to The Lodge where Sibyl and Katie, a young nurse, cared for him.

But if Sibyl ever felt imposed upon by the burdens of her household, she never complained. Solicitous of everyone's welfare she fluttered about fussing over them all, a plump comforting fixture at The Lodge.

After gorging on Sibyl's hot, melt-in-the-mouth cinnamon rolls, Adria and Kandy went directly to Kandy's father's room. Adria always dreaded this part of her recent visits to the spacious Graham home. Tears rose in her throat as she advanced into the large, red-carpeted bedroom and went to lay her cheek against her uncle's withered face.

Benjamin Graham's condition, thin face drawn to one side, lips chalky, paralyzed completely on one side and unable to speak words that could be understood, filled Adria with anguish. Uncle Benjamin had been a vibrant, eloquent man, respected and honored.

He clutched her warm hand in a claw-like grip and made an inarticulate sound in his throat. The twisted grimace on his paralyzed face was the closest he could come to the hearty smile of the past. Adria was vastly relieved when Kandy sank down on an ottoman at his feet and began to chat. Adria moved back and feeling a chair behind her, lowered herself into it.

Kandy was telling her father that Adria was taking a few days off to rest and about Gentry, the stranger they had stopped to help.

"As soon as he comes back I'll bring him to meet you," Kandy finished. "Now, I had better go get Adria 'squared away'." They kissed him and slipped out.

"I miss Sarge," Adria said when they were unpacking her suitcase a few minutes later in the spare bedroom next to Kandy's.

"Tell me about it!" Kandy said emphatically. "It's like getting by without my right arm. I'm to pick him up at the vet's this afternoon. The only one who won't be glad to see him is Sibyl. She's never quite come to grips with having a dog running about in her spotless house."

"Some people just don't care for dogs," Adria said. "But I wish I lived in the country where I could have one!"

Chapter 5

After lunch Adria wandered out to the back porch and then ambled across the back yard. To her left the last of Sarah's vegetable garden — turnips, green onions, carrots and beets — showed green against the tilled earth. Late blooming flowers of many hues thrust their colorful heads above a low stone border on her right. The Lodge housekeeper could make anything grow.

As she sauntered on out the back gate and began to climb up the pasture path toward the trees, Adria smiled contentedly. It's so peaceful here, away from the rush of traffic and people in the city. Maybe I should find work up here and get away from all the hassle of city life, she thought.

The Lodge had always been a refuge to her. When she was trying to recover from the deaths of both parents in a small plane accident, she had fled here. Not just the arms of Kandy's family had enclosed her in a cocoon of love, but even the old log house had seemed to hold her close, comforting and soothing her anguish.

And how many times had she retreated here after Giles had gone out of her life so abruptly and with such finality? She had thought she would die at first — and many times wished she could. Life without Giles had seemed utterly impossible.

Then Kandy had accepted the Lord in a little church in Taos and had then introduced Adria to Him. That was when Adria had begun to live again, immersing herself in her job and her new life in God. Adria had found a small but loving church in Albuquerque. The love and concern of her new church family had reached out to her as she struggled to start life anew. So she managed to go on — and even had begun to enjoy life again.

Adria was climbing steeply now following a narrow, rocky path that wound between huge trees and encroaching underbrush. The hum of insects and the scolding of a jaunty squirrel caressed her ear-drums. Birds flitted busily overhead, singing and chirping. She paused to watch a mountain bluebird drop to a branch of a pine tree, a grasshopper dangling from its bill.

Moving on, she felt anxiety drop away. Finally, panting, Adria dropped to a large rock beside the path to get her breath. Maybe I'm getting out of shape, she mused. I used to climb this path with Giles talking and laughing, and we never rested once.

She had met Giles in her junior year of college and his senior year. Their friendship had gradually ripened into a deep, satisfying love. There was nothing Adria had not been able to discuss with Giles. At the time she was sure he felt the same. They had shared their deepest feeling, heartaches and triumphs.

After Giles went away to do a stint in the military and even after he went to South America, they had written often, making plans for marriage as soon as Giles was released from his military duty.

When had things changed? With her chin cupped in her hands, Adria went over the last few letters she had received from Giles. She had done this a hundred times or more. Giles had not openly said he was involved in a secret operation, but Adria suspected he was when he abruptly began to avoid any mention of his activities or his whereabouts.

Then for three months she had received no mail at all and had almost gone out of her mind with worry. When at last he wrote, he only said he hadn't been allowed to write and hoped she had not been too worried.

Had there been another girl and Giles had just been trying to think of a way to break it off with Adria? After all, he had been far from home and it wasn't an uncommon thing for lonely American servicemen to seek comfort in the companionship of foreign girls. And sometimes a casual companionship ripened into more.

Adria had received two more letters, filled with his love for her. They had puzzled her at the time, tender but almost desperate in their intensity, as if he were pleading for her love — a love that he should know was assured.

Then the final one had come. It contained only a few lines. She knew them by heart. Tears prickled behind her eyelids as she squeezed her eyes tightly together and tried to shut out those tormenting words:

Adria, I sincerely regret that I must write this letter to you. Our marriage would never work. I'm sorry. Please forget me and get on with your life. Giles

That had been close to two years ago and even though Adria had written several times — she shuddered at her shamelessness — Giles had never written again. It was as if he had dropped from the face of her world. She presumed he had returned home to the states but she didn't even know that.

Like her cousin Kandy, Giles had also planned to go into forestry work. Kandy had checked, at Adria's insistence, if Giles had applied for forestry work anywhere in New

Mexico, and had come up with an absolute blank.

Adria got up and began climbing again. I must forget Giles, she thought. I must! And yet, she had told herself that innumerable times — and so had Kandy and other friends. If only she could! She had dated young men, eligible, interesting young men, but they never seemed to strike a chord in her heart.

"Dear God," she prayed, "help me forget Giles, and dear Jesus, if only you would help me to find out where he is — what happened to him. I just need to know!"

Adria pulled herself up a steep bit of trail by the branch of a tree. She now stood near a big rock. Above her was the hidden entrance to a cave. Bushes and trees crowded close to its mouth. She scrambled up to a small ledge. Pushing aside a large bush Adria stooped, and crouching low she slipped inside the shadowy cave depths.

Snapping on her flashlight, Adria took several crouching steps down a low, rough walled, narrow passageway before she straightened up. Standing slowly to her feet, she cast the powerful light about the cave-room. It picked up the wall about fourteen feet away and then revealed the narrow tunnel which led to smaller rooms beyond.

Where she stood was about sixteen feet wide and much taller than her head.

She and Kandy had come here nearly all their lives for picnics and even overnight campouts. When she met Giles, he had joined them and later when they grew closer, they had often come here alone to eat, talk and dream of their future together.

A dim light filtered into the cave from a crevasse under a cliff near the ceiling. Smoke from campfires was sucked out of the cave through that opening and diffused into the trees and brush beyond.

Adria located a couple of old blankets and pillows cached in an old foot locker she and Kandy had brought here years before. Seating herself upon their softness, pillows to her back, she willed her mind into a complete void.

Except for a subdued sound of birds and insects outside and the sighing of a faint breeze beyond the entrance, silence reigned. After a few minutes, Adria grew very drowsy. Stretching out on her back, with her head on the pillows, she was soon sound asleep.

She dreamed. She could hear Giles's voice in her dream, distinctly. It came from way back in the cave, echoing hollowly, he was calling her. She tried to answer but couldn't make a sound. She tried to go to him but her limbs seemed weighted as if in irons.

How long she lay struggling to speak and move, Adria did not know, but suddenly she awoke, drenched with perspiration. Her heart was pounding as she sat up and looked around in the dim light. Had her dream awakened her or had something else?

She searched the room with wide, distended eyes. She saw nothing. The nightmare had been so real that she was still feeling the effects of it, she told herself sternly.

"See," she scoffed at herself aloud. "There is no one here. Don't be so wimpy." But her flesh and spirit seemed to cringe with dread and fear that was rapidly turning into panic and terror.

Suddenly her mind jumped to a new thought. Could that unknown man who followed her like a shadow have followed her up here too? Was he back in the cave, watching her every move?

If he was, she was alone with him! The fearsome thought galvanized her into action. Jumping up, Adria tore across the room. Plunging into the short entrance tunnel, she didn't stoop low enough and bumped her head painfully on the low roof in her haste to get outdoors.

Once outside, she slid down to the path and ran to the first twist in the trail and stopped. Breathing hard and feeling the cool wind pressing her damp shirt against her hot body, she willed herself to stand still and listen.

It was totally silent here — as if the earth was holding its breath and listening too. Adria drew in a shuddering breath of relief. "No one was there," she told herself resolutely.

Then a new thought struck through her like the sharp thrust of a sword: It is too quiet! Even the sounds of birds and insects near the entrance had stilled. When she had come up, it had not been quiet like this! Had someone been out here and frightened the birds in his noisy flight to keep her from seeing him?

There! Even as she listened a chirp of a bird came and then a cicada began to sing again. A flash of silver arched out from a tree and landed in a taller one and began to peal out warbling sounds.

Fear beat in Adria's heart like a drum. Someone — or something — had been outside the cave. Perhaps it was only a wild animal but she had better get back to the house now! She had little fear of wild animals but the two-legged kind was a different story!

On legs like mush, Adria began a rapid descent toward the house, sliding and slipping over the loose rocks and pebbles. Once she fell but she didn't stop to see how badly she was hurt until she stood at the back gate.

With her stomach quivering and the muscles in her legs jumping from exertion, she looked back up the trail. No movement showed there. Had anything really been up there, or was it all a reaction to her very real nightmare?

The awfulness of it was she didn't know.

Chapter 6

As Adria stood near the gate, she heard voices near the barn. Several horses were stabled there. A pole fence surrounded the barn on three sides. She saw the back of Kandy's dark head and heard her quick laughter. Leaning on the fence next to her was Gentry Howard.

Adria moved quickly toward them, favoring her left leg. Hearing her step, her cousin and Gentry straightened and turned toward her. "I wondered where you had wandered off to," Kandy said lightly. Then her eyes widened with alarm. "What's wrong! Are you hurt?"

Kandy hurried to meet Adria, "You're limping! What happened?"

Sudden tears misted Adria's eyes but she tried to laugh off her cousin's concern. "Nothing's wrong — really. I just fell asleep in the cave and had a nightmare."

"A nightmare hurt your leg? Powerful nightmare!" Kandy scoffed.

Wiping the dampness from her eyes self-consciously with the heels of her hands, Adria tried to laugh. "I just woke up scared and imagined there was someone in the cave with me."

"And you came boiling out of there and slid all the way down the mountain!" Kandy finished.

"That's about it," Adria said. Exploring the top of her head with shaky fingers, she flinched. "It feels like I raised a king-sized bump on my head but I don't think it's even cut. I tried to raise the entrance ceiling with my head and it didn't work!"

"Are you sure someone wasn't up there?" Gentry spoke for the first time. His hazel eyes were intent on her face.

"I-I don't think so," Adria said slowly. "But I'm not sure."

"That land up there belongs to us," Kandy explained to Gentry. "It's unlikely anyone was there. It's fenced and posted against trespassers."

"But people sometimes ignore signs," Gentry said. "I'll be glad to go up and look around."

"No — I don't imagine there was anyone there," Adria said quickly. She moved to a wooden swing strung from a branch of a towering cottonwood tree and sank down. Pulling up her left trouser leg, she cringed. Blood was seeping from an ugly abrasion below her left knee. "Strange how the sight of your own blood makes you queasy," she managed lightly.

"We'd better disinfect that cut," Kandy said. "And then I think you'd better lie down for a while. You look shaken up."

"I'm fine, really I am," Adria demurred. "I just scared myself silly is all. A fine investigative reporter I am! I think I'd be a better fiction writer, I've got such a good imagination."

"But you can't be really positive it was just your imagination," Gentry said gravely. "I still think I should go up there and take a look."

"Thanks, but I don't really think it's necessary," Adria said, her blue-gray eyes touched his briefly and then looked away. "A strange man has been following me around lately down in Albuquerque and so the first thought I had when I woke up from that scary dream was that he had followed me up here too."

Alarm was mirrored in Gentry's eyes, "Is there a possibility that he did?"

"I don't think so," Kandy answered him. "This cousin of mine only let me get five hours sleep last night so we could sneak off long before the sun was up. Even Adria's admirer wouldn't get up at that ghastly hour!"

"And we didn't see a sign of him when we left, so I'm sure we gave him the slip," Adria said. Her own words lifted her feelings. "Now, I'll go douse my wound with antiseptic and I'll be almost as good as new!"

"By the way, did you get your car fixed," she asked Gentry.

"Sure thing! That little shriveled-up handyman of yours is a whiz. He fixed the car with a part that didn't even cost me much. He wouldn't let me pay him either. Acted mad when I insisted."

Kandy chuckled, "That's Fritz all right. He's a marvel in this commercial world. He and his wife Sarah, our housekeeper, have a comfortable little apartment in the back of our house and he is perfectly content to take care of the grounds and orchard and other chores. He says that 'things' can own a person and he doesn't like to be owned."

"We have to insure our possessions and clean and fix them all the time too," Adria said. "Maybe Fritz is the smart one."

"We'd better get your leg fixed up," Kandy told Adria.

As they started toward the house, Adria's mind retraced itself to her nightmare in the cave and to her intense feeling that someone had been watching her. Had someone really been there?

She slowly went over what had transpired step by step. She had panicked and rushed from the cave, striking her head painfully on the exit tunnel. Then there was that moment outside the cave when she realized how quiet it was — not even an insect or bird sound. Surely someone dashing outside had caused that sudden hush.

Then a new thought flitted into her mind. Of course! She, Adria, with her mad rush outside, had stilled the birds and insects! How stupid of her to think it was anyone else.

She hurried inside the house with a lightened heart.

Chapter 7

Dinner that night was a gala affair. Larry Graham, Kandy's brother, had been delighted to meet Gentry and made him welcome. As Adria watched her cousin, his deep blue eyes alight with life as he told a story of some amusing happening at work, she felt pride rise up like a ball of tears in her throat. Larry had always been such a lovable guy but until recently had been a miserable failure at everything.

How well she recalled those stormy sessions between Larry and his father. One could hear their raised voices all over the house. His father — a successful, respected and wealthy criminal attorney — could never understand Larry's failure at everything he tried. He wouldn't stick with college, the three small businesses his father had underwritten were total flops. He had even tried marriage and had a small child and ex-wife to support.

Shortly before Benjamin Graham's stroke, Larry had tried to get his father to finance a small gift and jewelry shop in Taos but had been adamantly refused. Somehow Larry had come up with a loan to begin the

48

business and it appeared to be thriving. Adria wondered idly who had supplied the money for Larry. Anyone who knew Larry considered him a poor credit risk. He had never paid his bills consistently. She recalled that in the past his ex-wife had threatened to take him to court to collect child support for their six-year-old daughter.

Adria brought her attention back to what Gentry was saying. "I have never taken a vacation, so after our business is transacted tomorrow, Larry, I'm off for two whole weeks."

"Never had a vacation?" Adria said. "You must have a slave-driver boss!"

"You can say that again!" Gentry said. "But things have changed. I now have shares in the company and my first vacation."

"Gentry, if you plan to spend it here you are more than welcome to stay right here at The Lodge," Larry said.

But Gentry was shaking his head. "Thanks, Larry, that's very kind of you but I don't want to inconvenience you. I've already made a reservation at an inn."

"But we insist," Larry said earnestly. "We have room to spare and we want you to stay. Cancel your reservation."

"You've been more than kind to invite me

for tonight," Gentry objected. "I plan to spend at least a week here and that's too long to impose on anyone, especially someone I just met today."

"We really would like you to stay," Kandy said.

Sibyl spoke warmly, "Young man, we want you to stay. It will be much more pleasant for you to stay with friends. Maybe Kandy can take off a little time and she and Adria can show you around."

"I'm almost sure I can get off for a few days," Kandy said eagerly. "And we'll try not to drag you to anything you don't wish to see."

Adria was surprised to see that Kandy's dark blue eyes were shining. The Kandy who was married to her job offering to leave it to take a man sightseeing!

Gentry's green eyes moved slowly over the group at the table, "You are mighty convincing. I'll admit it's lonesome sightseeing alone."

"Then it's settled," Sibyl said. "I always enjoy company. What kind of desserts do you like? I'm the baker around here."

Gentry's face registered dismay and he raised a large hand in protest, "I don't want to be a lot of bother."

"Sibyl makes the best desserts in New

Mexico," Kandy declared, "and she looks for chances to try her goodies on new people. You'll be her slave for life when you try her fried pies!"

"And her coconut pie and brownies," Adria said.

"Southern pecan! You can't beat that sister of ours' pecan pie anywhere," Larry exclaimed.

Sibyl's round face grew pink, "That's enough, you children!" But she looked pleased.

After the meal, Kandy made a call and returned jubilant. "I worked a week of my vacation so Coleen could have a week off in the spring. Now she's agreed to take my place while I take a week now."

"That's great," Gentry said. He turned to Adria, "Am I to have the honor of two lovely lady escorts to see Taos?" Adria darted a glance at Kandy and saw her face go still and a little tense. She really likes this guy, Adria thought in amazement. Personally, she had seen many men more handsome than Gentry Howard but if Kandy liked him, she would steer as clear of him as possible.

"Thanks, but I imagine I'd be poor company," Adria said quickly. "I think I'll mainly hike in the woods and read."

"Say, I don't want to horn in if you and your cousin had plans," Gentry protested.

But both Adria and Kandy assured him they had made no plans at all.

"I really do need to just rest and relax while I'm here," Adria said sincerely. "I feel myself getting downright paranoid like I was at the cave this afternoon. I need to get my nerves back together."

"It won't hurt a thing that you will be gone from your apartment for a while," Kandy said. "Maybe that admirer of yours will think you have moved out of town."

"What admirer?" Larry asked. "Is some guy giving you a bad time down there in the big city, Adria?"

After she and Kandy had told Larry about Adria's lanky protector, Adria turned to Kandy, "I do have one request, though. Now that you have brought Sarge home, can I take him with me when I go into the woods?"

"You know you can," Kandy said. "He'll be ecstatic."

"If that guy did happen to follow me up here, I would feel safer with Sarge with me."

"Sarge will take a plug out of him if he gives you any trouble," Kandy said. Her face became grave, "Do be careful though,

Adria. That guy seems awfully obsessed with you."

"I will be careful but I really don't think he can find me here. I've never even told my landlord where I go when I come up here. Anyway, with Sarge along I won't be afraid of anyone."

"That man who attacked Kandy is still on the loose too," Sibyl said. "I don't like the idea of you going in the forest alone, even with Sarge."

"I appreciate your concern, Sibyl," Adria said fondly, "but I suspect your forest is much safer than the streets of Albuquerque. I'm not afraid but I'll be careful."

Her words were confident but she felt a ripple of unease slide over her. She wasn't really afraid of the man who attacked Kandy. That had happened far away from The Lodge. But she was uneasy about the strange man who shadowed her as she moved around Albuquerque.

Who was he? Why did he seem to feel a need to protect her, even to see her safely to bed each night. Would he really harm her? If only he would let her talk to him, find out what made him tick. Was he a sane sensible man who in some way was attracted to her? Or was he a crackpot who considered her his girlfriend? That sort of person could be dangerous. If only she knew who and what he was!

Since the next day was Sunday, they all decided to attend church with Kandy, except Larry who kept his shop open on Sundays. Even Sibyl went when she found out their guest was attending. Afterward, when Gentry wanted to take them all out to lunch she said to Gentry, "Sarah's making southern fried chicken and will be upset if we don't go home to eat it. And Fritz is cranking up some homemade ice cream."

The meal was every bit as good as Sibyl had promised and they were all so replete that they just lazed around the remainder of the day. They took a short walk in the cool of the evening, watched a little TV, and then sat on the porch and talked until bed time.

"This is one of the most enjoyable days I have spent in a long time," Gentry said as they said good night.

As Adria dressed for bed, she also felt peaceful and relaxed. This is going to do me good, she thought. Up here I can forget about that spooky man down in Albuquerque. Maybe I can even finally put my relationship with Giles in the right perspective.

That ranger Kandy had introduced her to

the last time she was here seemed really nice and had asked her out. They had a good time and he had wanted to see her again; had asked her to call when she came back to Taos. Maybe she would.

She climbed into bed smiling. Or maybe I'll date that reporter who keeps asking me out. She chuckled as she reminded herself why she hadn't before. He was her employer's son and she had been afraid if she went out with him it might damage her relationship with her co-workers. She wanted no favors from anyone, especially the boss's son.

Jay was a little cocky but he worked hard at his job. She summoned his face into memory: curly black hair — she wondered if he permed it — teasing, dark-brown eyes, not really handsome but with a fantastic grin and the girls were crazy about him.

Then suddenly, without warning another face erased Jay's good looking face from her mind. Dark-brown hair, a little long that curled at the neck, a hawk-nose, dark skin stretched over ruggedly sculptured features. A slash like a knife cut on one side of his face when he grinned. Even his voice echoed in her mind whistling "I Dream of Jeannie with the Light Brown Hair," his song to her. Giles!

"Go away, Giles," she said crossly. "I want to forget you!" But did she really? Her fingers longed to touch the crisp hair that curled upon his collar. Even the memory of his crooked grin set her heart to beating crazily.

She pulled the pillow over her head. "Go away, Giles! I'm going to forget you up here in the forest! Go away and leave me alone!"

But it was a long time before sleep finally erased his image from her mind. And then she dreamed that crazy dream again, that he was calling her repeatedly and she lay leaden, unable to move a muscle to help him.

Chapter 8

The next morning after breakfast, Adria struck out up the mountain. A small pack on her back contained a sumptuous lunch, a book, flashlight, camera and a leash for Sarge.

As she let Sarge out ahead of her and closed the back gate, Adria smiled, remembering Kandy's relieved grin when Adria had adamantly insisted that she needed solitude instead of traipsing about Taos sightseeing with Gentry and Kandy.

Adria knew from the talk last night that Gentry had brought some new designs of turquoise jewelry for Larry to see. Gypsy Blue jewelry was widely known for its superb workmanship by skilled Indian artisans. They also sold fine Indian pottery and other Indian art. Larry stocked them in his gift shop, Blue Corn Treasures. After Gentry and Larry concluded their business, Kandy and Gentry planned to sightsee for the balance of the day.

She sobered a little as she mused. Kandy seemed really smitten with Gentry. The man seemed like a good man. She recalled Gentry's courteous and kindly manner when Kandy had taken him in to meet her father last night.

If Kandy is falling for Gentry I hope he feels the same way, she worried. But Kandy is a sensible girl, surely she won't fall too hard unless Gentry gives her encouragement. Love did strange things to people, though. Adria had always considered herself sensible but she definitely wasn't when it came to Giles Hughlet!

Mist hung heavy over the mountain, shrouding the trees with a shifting, blinding mass of white. Sarge bounding ahead, was quickly lost in its folds. When she called him back, he came reluctantly but obediently, tongue hanging out, dark eyes dancing with delight. There was nothing Sarge loved more than a run in the woods.

Clipping the leash from her pack onto Sarge's collar, Adria spoke softly, "I know you want to run and explore but when I get in the mist I'll be lost unless you wait for me. After the fog rises, you can be off the leash again. Okay?"

Sarge swiped a wet tongue over her cheek and then rubbed his head against her denim covered legs. She took his dark head between her palms and ruffled his fur. His expressive eyes radiated deep affection for her as he wriggled with pleasure.

They moved cautiously forward and in a couple of minutes were surrounded by mist — damp, but deliciously cool — giving the world an isolated unrealness. This morning Adria was at peace. She loved the forest. Stopping for a moment she closed her eyes, drinking in the damp piney odor tinged with the scent of earth and wild flower blossoms.

She could see only a step or two ahead now and sometimes not even that as they climbed slowly and cautiously upward through the shifting, swirling fog.

Twice they stopped to rest, she perched gingerly on a damp smooth boulder, and Sarge sitting on his haunches, ears and eyes alert, pink tongue lolling and dripping.

For some time they ascended slowly through the cold wet fog, their footsteps muted on the wet, slippery, sometimes needle-covered path. Suddenly Sarge stopped, his ears pricked up as he stared ahead, turning his head first one way and then the other, obviously listening to something she could not hear.

When he whined softly and started to move ahead again, Adria held him back. What did he hear? An animal, perhaps? Not a porcupine, she hoped. He had tangled with one once and had undergone the painful extraction of dozens of porcupine quills at the veterinary clinic. Since then he had hated porcupines with a passion and had to be sternly restrained by voice or leash whenever he saw one.

Sarge pulled at the leash and another soft eager whimper came from his throat. The fog had thinned slightly and Adria took a step forward when a sound caused her to halt. The indistinct sound, like the shuffle of a foot on gravel came again not far ahead. Sarge again pulled strongly against the leash in her hand but she held him back.

Then a soft trill began: breathtakingly beautiful bird-calls drifted dream-like from the mist. Then it melted into the whistled tune of a song she didn't know, hauntingly sad but enchanting. She stood completely still, captivated. The voice sounded like a man's. Sarge again tugged at the leash, a soft puppy-like whimper issued from his jaws. He acts like he knows the person, Adria thought. So it should be safe to go on.

Then the soft whistle changed and her heart gave a mighty lurch and then seemed to stop beating altogether. Trembling, her hand reached out to clutch at a tree trunk to steady herself. Softly the strains of "I Dream of Jeannie with the Light Brown Hair" floated from the mist, rising and falling in a sad, sweet cadence.

Giles! It had to be him. That had been Giles' song to her! Many times he had sung and whistled it to her. And he could do birdcalls too! It had to be Giles!

Adria didn't stop to think what Giles was doing here. That he was here was enough. Joy soared through her stunned being like a living flame. She tried to call but found she had almost lost her ability to speak in her shock, but on the second try her lips formed his name in a whisper of sound. On the third try, she called his name. It rang through the mist like a quivering bell chime.

Instantly the whistling stopped. Adria waited breathlessly for a long moment and then eagerly called his name again. The mist seemed hushed as if waiting. Why didn't Giles answer her call?

As if in a trance, she heard Sarge whining again as he surged against the restraint of the lead. She spoke to him softly but sternly. The total stillness wrapped itself about her like the enveloping fog.

Suddenly she was angry. She knew Giles was out there. Why didn't he speak? This was utterly ridiculous! "Giles," she snapped out angrily, "I know you are there! Answer me!"

There was an indistinct sound as if a foot had scraped a rock, then she heard hushed but definite sounds of footsteps moving rapidly away from them up the path.

Adria stamped her foot in frustration and fury, "Giles, I know that's you! Come back and talk to me!"

There was no sound now and Adria called furiously, "Giles! Why are you doing this to me." There was no answer and suddenly her legs seemed to lose all strength and she sank upon the ground, drawing Sarge down with her. She felt hot tears on her icy face.

For long moments she sat on the rough rocky ground but did not feel the dampness seeping through her jeans and shirt. She felt shocked and numb and drained. After a few minutes, Sarge whined and licked at her wet cheeks, his warm eyes puzzled upon her face.

She tried to stand and found that partial strength had returned to her limbs. Stumbling, she began slowly to climb again, following Sarge's eager straining body. Pain, like a physical hurt, flooded through her being. Why did Giles reject her like this? Why? Why?

Then anger again lashed her raw heart. Coward! Coward! Did he not have the nerve to face her after casting her aside like a worn out shoe?

"I hate you, Giles!" her cold lips spat out.

But her heart denied her words. Angrily, she acknowledged that her very being ached to see Giles. Even if he rejected her to her face! If only she could see him, feel the touch of his strong brown hands again.

Even if they were pushing her away? No, she could not bear that either! "What a mixed up fool I am," she muttered to herself.

She suddenly became aware that they had arrived at the cave. Turning her back to the mountain, she lifted her face to the soothing cold mist. As she stood, the fog thinned and she could see the sickly yellow light of the sun. As the moments passed, the mist slowly faded into drifting, dissipating scraps of cloud.

Reluctantly Sarge lay down beside her as she spread her sweater on a large rock and sat down. For a long while she sat in the golden, warming light of the sun and watched it melt away the fog until she could see the roof of The Lodge below her. She tried to put all thought from her troubled mind. Gradually calm came again to her.

Finally she allowed thoughts of the puzzling actions of the whistler to return. Was there a possibility that the man was not Giles? If not, then he had been a trespasser and most certainly would not wish to be found on private land. That could explain his running away. Besides, she admitted to herself rather sheepishly, if the man wasn't Giles, he might have thought her a raging imbecile.

Sarge moved restlessly and looked up at her pleadingly.

"We'll go in a little bit, Sarge," she said. "I just want to think about this some more. You knew the man, didn't you? You acted like it was someone you liked. And you liked Giles, didn't you?"

Sarge licked her hand and wagged his tail.

"But it wouldn't have been logical for Giles to not answer when I called him," she reasoned. Not the Giles she remembered. It just didn't make sense that he would run away like that. And if it was Giles, why would he be climbing around secretively on Graham land? The man must not have been Giles.

Sarge whined and licked her hand and she looked down at him. For a moment she saw only his beseeching eyes as she stroked his head, then slowly something else registered on her brain. In the scuffed dirt near her feet were tracks — men's athletic shoe tracks. Stooping, she looked more closely, pushing away Sarge's wet, licking tongue.

The whistler must have been sitting on

this rock when he was whistling and warbling bird-calls. From the rock the tracks led away up the trail, away from the hidden entrance to the cave above.

She stood quickly and began to climb up the trail, ignoring Sarge's imploring look to turn him loose. She didn't want him racing away. If she came upon the whistling stranger she didn't want to be alone.

But even though they followed the occasional traces of shoe tracks for almost an hour, she saw no one. Near the top of the mountain, Adria, panting for breath, finally gave up the search. She hadn't found any tracks for some time, so she presumed the man had left the trail somewhere.

Retracing their steps to the cave, Adria turned Sarge loose and he went bounding away. The sun was now hot, so she put down her sweater on a pine needle covered spot under a tall tree, leaning her back against its thick trunk. It felt good to rest.

The heavy scent of pine blended faintly with the perfume of wild flowers was intoxicating in her nostrils. In spite of her shock in the earlier part of the day, she was now relaxed and pleasantly tired. The warmth of the fresh, scented air and the faint sounds of insects and bees lulled her until she could hardly keep her eyes open.

A perky squirrel ran down a tree, but flicked his long tail and raced away when she raised her head to look sleepily at him. She curled up on the heavy sweater, the sound of birds and insects faded from her consciousness and she slept.

Much later she was jerked suddenly from sleep by Sarge's excited barking. Sitting up dazedly, she looked around and saw no one but could hear Sarge barking to her right, high above the cave. Quickly she scrambled to her feet and had opened her mouth to call him when his barking shut off abruptly.

Alarmed she called him loudly several times, ordering him to come to her. When he didn't come, she hung her pack on a limb of a nearby tree and scrambled as quickly as possible up the trail. When she was above the cave, she left the trail and angled toward where she had last heard Sarge. It was very steep and soon she was breathless and perspiring.

Her heart was pounding with dread and fear. Why didn't Sarge come to her? He was well-trained and very obedient. If she had let something happen to Kandy's dog, she would never forgive herself. Kandy loved him like a child.

Several times she called but he not only didn't come, he didn't bark or make a sound. Was he hurt? "Dear God," she prayed fervently, "don't let anything happen to Sarge."

Then suddenly Sarge was there, standing a short way above her on the mountain slope. When she spoke his name, he turned toward her and wagged his tail but then turned his handsome head to look up through the trees. He whined and took a step in that direction.

"Come to me, Sarge," Adria ordered more sharply than she usually spoke to him.

The German Shepherd whined low in his throat, then turned reluctantly and came to her side. She laid her hand on his head and he rubbed his head against her leg. Then he faced about and again whimpered softly as he gazed out into the dense wilderness of brush and trees above them on the mountain.

She ordered him to come with her and began a slipping, sliding diagonal descent back to the trail. Sarge came willingly enough but twice he stopped and looked back the way they had come and whimpered softly.

Whoever was back there was someone Sarge knew well and loved. Adria felt a quiver run through her body at the thought. The only ones she had known Sarge to love that way were Kandy and Giles. Others he knew and liked, including herself, but Kandy and Giles he had always idolized.

Had the whistler been Giles after all? Had he left the trail and gone over the mountain and Sarge had trailed and found him? It seemed preposterous. Yet — strange things were going on here. If it was Giles, why wouldn't he talk to her?

Chapter 9

Kandy strolled about her brother's gift shop. He and Gentry were talking business in Larry's small office at the back of the store. Pride grew in her heart as she moved about touching first one art object and then another. Larry had at last found his niche. Each piece of art looked hand picked for quality, workmanship and variety. The shop was named well — Blue Corn Treasures — because each item was a treasure.

The two display windows contained selected pieces of genuine handmade and hand painted Indian pottery from different tribes, copper craft, exquisite jewelry — some bearing the prestigious Gypsy Blue brand — and articles of leather, wood and stone. The treasures were displayed on a bed of white gravel. One window held a rough slab of rock on which was laid out a gorgeous array of silver jewelry, set with blue and green turquoise, ruby coral and other colorful stones which she didn't know.

Tucked here and there and displayed on the walls were ears of blue Indian corn, partly open to display the colorful kernels.

Everything was arranged tastefully and decoratively, utilizing the space well. Paintings and sculpture were also displayed. The shop was shining clean and a delight to browse in.

Kandy was studying a large painting on the wall of a wagon train strung out over a hill and into a plain beyond when Gentry spoke at her elbow. "That is beautifully done, isn't it?"

"Yes, it is," Kandy concurred. "I don't recognize the painter's name — Katrina Stone. See the detail of the face of that little ragged barefoot girl standing near the third wagon?"

Gentry leaned close to Kandy and looked intently at the child. "She's not a pretty child," he said slowly, "but her face is striking and looks so alive. Look at the expression on her face as she looks up at her father — pure adoration."

Kandy stood back and gazed at the picture. "You can see why. Her father looks so strong and fearless with that rifle over his arm as he looks back over the trail. She obviously feels very safe with her father protecting her."

Gentry was still scrutinizing the picture, "I almost feel that I've seen that face before. Do you suppose she was painted from a real child model?"

"I wouldn't be surprised," Kandy said. "She does look very real."

"Long black braids hanging down her back, dark brown eyes — almost black," Gentry was speaking softly, almost as if to himself, "and those straight dark eyebrows and short, straight nose."

Gentry turned to look full at Kandy, studying her face until Kandy felt her face begin to burn. "Why are you staring at me like that?"

Gentry didn't answer but swung back to examine the picture more closely, muttering, "Even the skin is the same. Amazing!"

"What? What?" Kandy said, beginning to be irritated. "What are you seeing that I don't see?"

"That girl's face is you," Gentry said, quickly turning excited green eyes upon Kandy.

"That can't be," Kandy protested, extremely embarrassed now. "Maybe it does resemble my face but. . . ."

"I'm serious," Gentry said. "Look, the nose is yours — short and straight, the brows are dark and straight. . . ."

"And the hair is black and straight too, just like mine," Kandy said with light sarcasm. "And the skin is as dark as an Indian's and the face is not pretty — just like mine!"

It was Gentry's turn to look embarrassed, "I never said you weren't pretty. I said that child's face wasn't pretty!"

"But you said the child was me," Kandy said impudently, for some contrary reason taking pleasure in his discomfort.

Gentry's face had taken on a pink tinge but he stood his ground. Patiently he spoke as if explaining to a child. "I know all girls want to be pretty — even beautiful — but believe me, I would rather one had character any old day!"

"Girls would disagree with you," Kandy said perversely. "Gentlemen never notice girls for their character, they notice them for how pretty they are." She realized suddenly that they were almost quarreling! How ridiculous — and over such a silly thing!

Gentry's face was no longer smiling. For a long moment he stared at Kandy and she felt her face growing hot again but she stubbornly refused to look away from those serious green eyes. "Not too long ago I thought I was in love with a girl who looked like an angel," he said softly. "I found out she was a devil. I'll always look closer than a face when I pick a girlfriend from now on."

Kandy laughed self-consciously, "I'm sorry about your disappointment in your girlfriend. And I'm afraid I was rude. I don't know what got into me, maybe we all have a little bit of the devil in us sometimes. Forgive me?"

Gentry's serious eyes continued to rest upon her, but his full lips slowly curved into a smile that moved to his eyes.

Kandy felt her heart beating strongly and she felt more than a little breathless. Why should this man's smile affect her so strongly. She, Kandy Graham, married to her job, her only real love a dog named Sarge! Sensible Kandy Graham, forest ranger, defender of wild-life.

She heard Gentry's voice again and pushed away her brooding thoughts.

"There's nothing to forgive," Gentry was saying earnestly. "I just wanted you to know that I wasn't deprecating you in any way. From the first time I laid eyes on you I felt you were someone I wanted to know better."

Kandy didn't know how a girl usually answered such admissions — if this wasn't just a "line" — so she spoke honestly, and was horrified afterward wondering if he would think her too forward, "I liked you from the first too."

"Good," Gentry said, to Kandy's vast relief, "Let's get out of here and go find something to drink before we start making like tourists."

Larry called goodbye from the office doorway as they started out the door into the bright New Mexico sunlight, "Come back here at one o'clock and I'll buy you tourists lunch."

"We'll take you up on that!" Gentry called back.

A few minutes later they were seated at a shady corner table in a patio enclosed by adobe walls, lined with flower boxes. A tinkling fountain stood in the center, the sunlight turning the falling droplets into sparkling jewels.

A pretty waitress came quickly. "Would you like a menu?"

"Do you want something to eat or just a drink?" Gentry asked Kandy.

"Just something to drink. I'll save my appetite for the lunch my brother is buying us."

"We have some very good wines," the waitress suggested.

"No alcoholic beverages," Gentry said firmly, then looked quickly at Kandy, "at least I don't want one. You are welcome to have one, of course."

"No, I'd rather have a fresh limeade."

Gentry ordered the same and when the

waitress moved away, he gazed at Kandy earnestly for a moment. The man had such a disconcerting way of looking at her — like he was trying to see inside her mind — that set her pulses to racing!

"I might as well tell you from the start," Gentry said, "I'm a Christian."

Kandy felt laughter bubbling up within her. It was almost as if he was confessing to a crime! "I might as well tell you something right off too," Kandy said, trying to keep a straight face. "I'm also a Christian. Have been for a couple of years." Astonishment and then delight spread over Gentry's face. "Say that's great!"

Kandy's eyes glinted with mirth, "You declared yourself a Christian like I was going to consider you far out or something."

Gentry grinned and looked slightly embarrassed, "I've only been a Christian for a few weeks and I thought all my friends and business associates would be delighted and want some of the same. It was a rude awakening. They wanted no part of it!"

He grimaced, "Perhaps I came on a little too strong but I found out real quick that lots of people think Christians are fanatics and pretty weird." He chuckled, "I suppose I am a little fanatical. But being a Christian is the most wonderful thing that ever happened to me. I just can't help being excited."

Kandy leaned toward Gentry and spoke softly, "I was attacked and beaten pretty badly by a wild-eyed hoodlum two years ago. It was through that experience that I met Jesus. After the attack, my body healed and wasn't even scarred much, but my mind was scarred. Nightmares and fears tormented me night and day."

"I'm so sorry," Gentry said gently. "It must have been horrible for you!"

"I nearly went out of my mind," Kandy said. "I found myself studying the face of every man I saw looking for my attacker. I couldn't sleep at night and was afraid to be alone — thinking he might return and finish me off."

"The man was never found?"

"No, and the police could never find a motive for the beating. I had never seen the man before and haven't since."

"There are a lot of people out there who are stoned on drugs and alcohol. . . ."

Kandy was shaking her head, "No, I don't think this man was doped up on drugs. His eyes were as normal as anybody's until he began beating me. Then they turned wild, like a fire out of control. He looked like he enjoyed the pain he was inflicting on me, like he was getting a crazy high from it.

"That's why we almost didn't stop to help you yesterday," Kandy admitted. "I never stop to help people anymore. The man pretended to be having car trouble, out on a forest road. I stopped to help him and without a word of explanation he just started to work me over."

"How utterly awful for you." Gentry's lips pressed into a tight, grim line. "That brings out the murder in a man!"

"In this woman's heart too," Kandy admitted. "For weeks I felt like taking a shotgun and going man hunting!"

The waitress brought their drinks and as they sipped the frothy lime drinks, Gentry asked, "You came to know the Lord through that experience?"

"Yes, even though I had always gone to church sporadically, I never had seen a need for God in my life. Dad was a strong protective father, and my sister Sibyl was always there for me, so I never felt a need for God. The rampant fears and nightmares were inside me where neither Dad nor Sibyl could reach."

"Perhaps there has to come a traumatic experience for many of us to feel a need for Christ," Gentry said.

"That may be so. In my case it was certainly that way. When a few trips to a psychologist didn't seem to help, in desperation I finally decided to try church. I went to a new church, directed by God, I'm sure, and found some very caring Christians who not only led me to the Lord but drew me into the church family. They literally loved me back to mental health."

"That's fantastic," Gentry said. "I'm afraid my conversion wasn't spectacular like that but it's still very real to me. My brother Elliott and his wife Lee are both such living examples of Christ that they just made me hungry for God. I haven't known Christ long but He has revolutionized the way I look at life."

"It's amazing, isn't it?" Kandy said softly. "Think of what we missed out on for so long."

Gentry raised his head and stared into space, his eyes far away, "The owner of Gypsy Blue Enterprises put me through college so I could go back and manage the business. When I was actually manager, I thought I had reached the zenith, the absolute pinnacle in my life. I lived and breathed the business."

He brought his eyes back to Kandy's face. "After I accepted the Lord as Savior, I realized how empty and shallow my life had been. My whole life had been tied up with perishable pottery and jewelry! I still enjoy my part in the business — I even own a part of it now — but Jesus, and people, are far more important to me now."

"I heartily agree." Suddenly Kandy glanced at her watch and exclaimed, "Say, it's ten o'clock! We'd better get busy or we won't see anything before one o'clock."

For the next three hours, Kandy and Gentry wandered through the narrow, crowded streets, visiting the unique little shops and strolling through the plaza. They visited the courtyard of Kit Carson's home and museum and examined an old ox-cart and bee-hive clay oven.

At nearly one o'clock, they turned their steps toward Blue Corn Treasures. Somewhere during the morning Gentry had casually taken Kandy's slim brown hand in his large one and it had seemed as natural as rain to stroll hand in hand the balance of the morning.

As they came near the corner where the tile-roofed, adobe shop stood, they saw Larry step out the side door preceded by a tall blond-bearded man. For a moment they stood near each other, obviously arguing. A group of tourists ambled past the two and for a couple of moments they were hidden. Gentry and Kandy were just a few steps away when the group moved on and she could again see her brother and the blond stranger.

Larry had now moved back into the store but he said something to the man before he shut the door in the stranger's face. Larry's face had been twisted in anger. The bearded man stood staring at the closed door for a brief moment and then he swung around abruptly and almost collided with Kandy and Gentry.

As the blond man's icy blue eyes met Kandy's, she clutched convulsively at Gentry's arm. Savage blue fire — as cold as a north wind — seemed to leap out of the man's eyes as he stared malevolently into Kandy's face. The mouth was curled into a slightly mocking grin.

Terror lanced through her, gripping her mind in a paralyzing iron fist and setting the muscles in her stomach to trembling. The strength melted from her limbs and she would have fallen had she not been holding onto Gentry's arm.

The man strode swiftly away down the block without looking back, turned the corner and disappeared. Clinging to Gentry's arm, Kandy watched him out of sight in stupefied silence.

She suddenly became aware that Gentry

was calling her name anxiously and was asking her what was wrong. Dazedly she looked up into his green concerned eyes.

"That was the man," she whispered, "who attacked me two years ago!"

"Are you sure?" Gentry asked incredulously.

"I'm sure," Kandy quavered. "He's wearing a beard now but I would know those eyes anywhere. They-they terrify me!"

"Do you think the man recognized you?"

Kandy was shaking and Gentry put a strong, steadying arm around her shoulders.

"I'm positive he recognized me," Kandy said. A shudder ran over her body and Gentry tightened his arm about her.

"He isn't going to hurt you," Gentry said. "I'll see to that!"

"Thanks," Kandy said and drew in a deep, quivering breath. "Just give me a moment, I'll be all right."

Gentry turned to look at the closed side door of Blue Corn Treasures and then back at Kandy. His voice was grim when he spoke, "Maybe your beating wasn't just a random attack. That man and your brother know each other. I think we'd better talk to Larry and get some answers to this puzzle."

Chapter 10

Adria looked at her watch. It was nearing noon but suddenly she had no desire to eat her lunch in the cave as she had planned. Her fright of the evening before and the odd experience with the whistler, which might or might not have been Giles, had left her a little wary of being in an enclosed space alone.

She glanced up at the cave. A shiver ran down her spine. Was it possible that the whistler was using the cave as a temporary home? The thought was a little scary. She turned to start away and then paused.

"I hate to be scared off," she said aloud. "I'm going in that cave and see if anyone is there. Then I'll know!"

She called Sarge to her side and attached the leash to his collar. "You'll protect me, won't you, boy?"

Sarge cocked his head to one side and barked sharply once. Adria laughed. "Thanks, Sarge, I knew you would!"

They climbed to the entrance to the cave and Adria pushed aside the concealing brush and stooped to enter. She was watching Sarge carefully, but although he sniffed at the entrance, he showed no alarm.

She recalled that after Kandy's attack by that wild-eyed stranger, she had sent Sarge to attack school. It was a comforting thought right now! The German Shepherd was large and heavy and would attack and hold on command. He was also trained to disarm a person on command. Adria knew all the signals.

I'm glad Kandy is with Gentry, she thought, or Sarge would be with her. It was seldom that Kandy was separated from her dog. Her supervisor even allowed him to accompany Kandy on the job, whether in the office or on forest trails and roads.

Adria and Sarge moved quickly through the low, narrow entrance. Stepping out into the large main room, she switched on the powerful flashlight and swept the walls with the beam. No one was here and the blankets and pillows she had left out in her haste the evening before were still lying in the same place.

She folded the two blankets and stowed them and the pillows in the foot locker. Then walking softly and with goose bumps prickling her arms, Adria crossed the large room and stood before the opening to the cells beyond. I might as well search the whole place while I'm at it, she thought.

Sarge snuffled about the narrow opening

but when she urged him forward, he showed no hesitation. Adria had to stoop to go through the short tunnel that led to the next room. No one was there either and so she moved to her right and knelt down and crawled through the next opening. The dog crawled ahead of her.

This room was very small, could hardly be called a room at all. Adria could almost touch all four sides standing in the center and the ceiling was so low in places she had to watch that she didn't bump her head. But she knew the compartment beyond this one was much larger.

Adria realized suddenly that she was breathing very shallowly and that her muscles were tensing until they ached. She drew in a deep breath and let it out slowly. Then she deliberately relaxed her muscles and stretched, breathing deeply. She felt better.

There was only one more room in the cave. To reach it, she would have to crawl for about ten feet. Kneeling, she flashed her light into the opening. There were no fallen rocks or snakes — or goodness only knows what else that might sometimes lurk in caves. She had never gone into these inner caves by herself before and she felt the hair lifting on the back of her neck at the thought of this longer crawl.

But she took another deep breath and determinedly got on her knees and sending Sarge before her, began crawling. This passageway was wide enough but with a rough, low ceiling. There was a bend about midway. By the time she had negotiated the turn and crawled out the other side, her heart was banging against her ribs and she had broken out in cold sweat.

Sarge eased out of the room ahead of her and she followed and stood up. By the light of the flash, she saw that Sarge appeared wary. She moved the light around the room but he stood in one place, lifting his head and sniffing the air.

Adria drew in a deep breath and sniffed, also. Did she detect a slight odor of tobacco? She was certain that she did.

Pale sunlight filtered in from a crack near the ceiling to light the room dimly, but she kept her flashlight on.

Suddenly Sarge started across the room. He came to the end of the leash and turned back to look at her inquiringly. When she followed him he walked warily, ears up and eyes alert and watchful, across the room and around a large boulder. Adria felt herself holding her breath.

The boulder had shut off a portion of the room from her view but now she saw what interested Sarge so much. This section was set up for camping!

A cot spread with a foam mattress and sleeping bag rested against one rough wall and a butane lantern and camp stove sat on a jutting rock at the end wall. On a ledge to her left were stacked canned foods, a small can of coffee, and a camping kit complete with skillet, coffee pot, cooking pan, metal cups, plates and flatware. Two canteens hung on pegs driven into a crack in the wall. They were heavy and sloshed when Adria shook them.

A case hung from another peg and when Adria took it down she found it contained expensive-appearing, high-powered binoculars.

Sarge padded over to the bed and snuffled. Adria moved to his side watching him closely. "Does this stuff belong to the guy we heard whistling, Sarge?" Adria said softly.

At the sound of her voice, Sarge wagged his tail but continued his investigation. Suddenly he poked his nose under the edge of the cot and sniffed noisily. Then he lay down and sampled the air under the bed with his nose, then pawed at something Adria could not see.

Quickly Adria got down on her knees and

directed the light under the bed. Her heart quickened when she saw a long case underneath. Pulling out the heavy object, she lifted it to the cot and snapped open the two catches. Flipping the lid back, Adria gasped.

Inside were two handguns, a .38 police revolver and a .357 Magnum. A rifle with a scope completed the cache.

She studied the rifle and decided — from the knowledge she had acquired from doing an article on hunting once — that it must be a .270 Winchester. All were shiny clean and well-oiled. A wicked-looking knife in a scabbard, a belt and holster, a shoulder holster and several boxes of shells also lay in the case.

Sarge sniffed the weapons and growled.

Adria felt panic rising in her throat. They had better get out of here! She and Sarge had stumbled onto more than a tramp's camp. Everything here was new-looking, clean, well arranged. The guns looked ominous and expensive.

Tensely, Adria stood still and listened. Her rapid breathing and Sarge's panting were loud in the silent room. Whoever was using this place as a hideaway must know that people seldom ventured into the back of the cave.

"Let's get out of here, Sarge," Adria said tensely. She could hardly restrain herself from plunging into the tunnel in headlong flight. Stay calm, she cautioned herself silently.

But she could not keep haste from her steps as she walked into the other part of the room and knelt at the low entrance to the passageway. Her heart was pounding wildly as she sent Sarge ahead of her into the tunnel. Her hands were cold and slippery on the flashlight as she followed on hands and knees.

A sharp stone bit into her left knee but Adria didn't pause. She was at the bend now and Sarge had disappeared around it. She crawled faster. Panic was beginning to hammer in her throat and she had trouble breathing. Close places had always made her claustrophobic and now near-panic was making it decidedly worse.

Fearful thoughts poured into her mind. What if they met the owner of those guns in one of these inner rooms where he skulked, waiting for them to emerge, weapon ready. Even courageous Sarge would not be a match for guns. They could both be hurt or killed in this isolated tomb-like cave!

"Adria," she scolded herself sternly, "you are being neurotic and scaring yourself silly.

You don't even know the person who is camping in the cave is a dangerous person. Having that strange character following you around in Albuquerque has gotten to your nerves."

With vast relief, Adria saw that during her lecture to herself, she had gone through the tiny room and crawled through into the larger one. Without a word from her, Sarge had already started through the next connecting passageway, looking back once to see if she was following. Thankfully, she could stand upright through this one and it was short.

When they came out into the large room a few minutes later, Adria glanced hastily about and made straight for the entryway.

Nothing ever felt better than when she stood once more by the large rock below the cave entrance and felt the hot sun on her face!

She put a caressing hand on Sarge's handsome head and spoke softly, "At least we found out what we wanted to know. Someone is camping in the cave. I might not have been too far-off when I felt someone looking at me yesterday evening. Someone could have been there." The thought sent a chill down her backbone.

"However," she said musingly to Sarge,

"the whistler didn't try to harm us in any way, and he is almost certainly the same person. So I have probably been making a very large mountain out of a very small ant hill."

Sarge gave a quick pleased bark as if answering her. She took off his leash and said lightly, "Let's go up to the gazebo and eat. I've had enough of caves for today!"

Sarge gave another happy bark and raced up the trail ahead of her. Shouldering her pack, Adria followed. As she climbed, her mind was busy.

What would anyone be doing camping out on the Grahams' private land? Perhaps a student or someone with limited resources seeing the country? Possibly, but that sounded unlikely. A person on foot, traveling across country, would not be able to carry all of that gear on his back.

A new thought intruded. Could her admirer from Albuquerque have followed her up here? Surely not! They had left very early and had seen no sign of him. Besides, she had never seen him in a vehicle. Of course, that didn't mean he didn't own one. Besides, why would he have three guns and a knife along?

She had turned onto another path now and was climbing steeply. Sarge had raced back and was now ahead of her on the gazebo path. She saw his waving tail disappear around a bend.

Giles! Her mind was back to the whistled songs and bird-calls. A quiver ran over her body as she recalled how "I Dream of Jeannie" had sounded so much like Giles's rendition. Could the mysterious stranger be Giles? He would be no stranger to weapons. She had never known what type of work Giles did but from his reticence she had presumed it was clandestine.

But if it was Giles, why all the secrecy, why come to Taos, and why hide out on Graham land? Was Giles in some kind of trouble? She could not imagine Giles doing anything illegal — not ever — but maybe he had gotten mixed up with people that he had to hide from. That's strictly TV stuff, she scoffed at herself.

Just ahead of her through the trees, she saw the gray roof of the ramada. For a few more breathless moments she climbed and then came out on a knoll. She sank down on a large boulder gasping for breath. Sarge came dashing back and lay down at her feet, his pink tongue lolling and his eyes dancing.

After a few moments of rest, Adria — with Sarge once more bounding ahead — walked down a dim path through the trees, rocks and brush until they came out onto a rocky cliff.

The gazebo was built on a point where the view was spectacular. Forest, like a sea of green velvet stretched as far as the eye could see below and on all sides. Far below, Adria could see the extensive shake roof of The Lodge. Between the trees, here and there, a silver ribbon could be seen winding down the mountainside to drop into a larger stream below.

Climbing the steps of the ramada, Adria deposited her pack on the picnic table and stretched out in a wooden lounge chair. She could hear the faint tinkle of water trickling over rocks nearby.

This is contentment, she sighed. A slight breeze soughed through the needles of a giant pine tree close behind the gazebo. A lone pine cone fell. Birds sang nearby and clouds floated serenely in the clear blue above.

When Sarge came rushing back, dripping from his splashing in the stream, instead of laying out their lunch, Adria had fallen sound asleep.

Chapter 11

Kandy and Gentry went around to the front entrance of the gift shop and proceeded immediately to the office.

The office door was closed but Kandy opened it quietly without knocking. Larry was sitting at his desk, his head bowed into his hands. For a long moment while they stood staring at him, he sat motionless. Finally he raised his head and looked at them. His face was ashy-gray and his eyes were dull and haggard.

"What's wrong, Larry," Kandy asked in alarm as she hurried to his desk.

Larry rose quickly to his feet, knocking an open ledger to the floor. He bent to retrieve it and when he straightened up there was a crooked grin on his handsome sculptured lips. "What do you mean?" he asked.

When Kandy continued to stare at him, he lifted a hand and brushed his forehead lightly, "I-I just haven't felt too well today. Maybe those peanuts I ate earlier didn't agree with me."

"Larry, we heard you having an argument with that big blond, bearded guy," Kandy said earnestly. "He upset you terribly. Was he threatening you?"

The color had come back into Larry's face now and his lopsided grin widened. "Kandy — what makes you think such a crazy thing. Of course he wasn't threatening me. He was just sore over a little bet I won off of him. And I got a little huffy too. That's all there was to it."

"I'm not sure I believe you," Kandy said slowly, "because I know that man. He's the one who beat me out on that forest road two years ago."

The pallor returned to Larry's face as he stood for a moment staring at Kandy. "That couldn't be true. You said you never saw the man but once. Surely you're mistaken."

Gentry was still standing by the door and he spoke now, "The man seemed to know your sister and Kandy's sure he's the man who attacked her."

Larry glanced at Gentry but again addressed his sister, "Kandy, you're imagining things. I know the man and I'm sure he would never do such a thing!"

"Who is he?" Kandy asked evenly.

"It's just a fellow I met at a party somewhere," Larry said. "I don't even remember where." His eyes didn't quite meet Kandy's. "It couldn't have been the same person. Didn't you say he was smooth shaven. I never saw this fellow without a beard."

"I would know his eyes anywhere," Kandy said. "I ought to, I saw them often enough in nightmares after the attack!"

"Lots of people's eyes are the same," Larry said, a note of impatience in his voice. "Forget it, Sis, that man was not the one who attacked you."

"He was!" Kandy's voice had risen a note and her eyes were stormy. "Why are you protecting that guy? Does he have something on you?"

"Kandy, I can't believe you are accusing a man of something with no better proof than that you recognized his eyes!"

"He also recognized me," Kandy said sharply. "As soon as he laid eyes on me a strange, weird light seem to flame up in his eyes. They were the same burning, mocking blue that taunted me as he was beating me!"

Larry lifted a defeated hand. "Okay, okay, we'll say he was the man who beat you. Are you going to the police? It would only be your word against his, but if you want to go, I'll go with you."

"Forget it," Kandy snapped. "You don't believe me so let's just drop it!"

Larry dropped his eyes for a minute and then said gently, "As I said before, I've not felt well today and with a difficult customer or so and book work to do, which I hate, I'm not myself today. I'm sorry to be so cantankerous." He looked up and grinned penitently, "Forgive me, Sis?"

Kandy studied his face briefly, then a grin tugged at her lips. It was hard to stay angry with likable Larry. Her voice was still slightly aggrieved as she said slowly, "It was my fault too. Maybe you are right, I'm probably imagining that your friend beat me up."

"He's not my friend," Larry said nonchalantly. "Just someone I met casually. However, in case there might be a vague possibility that guy was your attacker, it might be good to stay away from isolated places. Now, are you guys ready to eat?"

Larry took them to a little Mexican place on a side street where the food was excellent but Kandy noticed that he ate little. When she commented on his lack of appetite for the food he was usually very fond of, he shrugged it off. "Still got a bit of upset stomach."

Gentry, however, ate with every evidence of enjoyment. Larry was unusually quiet but Gentry was such an amusing table mate that Kandy scarcely noticed. Relaxed by Gentry's easy manner, Kandy soon forgot the morning's happenings. Although she didn't usually talk much about her life, Gentry soon had her relating funny and even sad accounts of her encounters with wild-life in the forest work she loved so much.

Larry didn't stay with them long. "I have a lot of work to do today," he said regretfully as he arose from the table. "Maybe we can go out one of these evenings soon to a really nice place."

Picking up the bill — over Gentry's protests — he started away, "You two have a good time and I'll see you this evening at home."

Gentry watched Larry hurry out, then turned to Kandy. "I would say that your brother is deeply troubled about something."

"Yes, I believe so too, but I have no idea what the problem is. I'm sure it has to do with that bearded young man, though, that he assured us he scarcely knew."

"He looked positively sick when we went into his office," Gentry said thoughtfully, "and not from some minor stomach upset, either."

Kandy looked into Gentry's concerned face and shook her head in consternation, "Larry acted scared — really scared. Something that happened just this morning has made a definite change in him."

"Right! He was whistling and cheerful this morning when he left for work, like he had the world by the tail on a downhill pull."

Kandy said thoughtfully, "Usually Larry is so easy going it's hard to make him angry. But he was really upset at that man. I didn't buy his story about their having an argument over a little bet. Larry has his faults but I never knew him to make a bet in his life."

"I don't know your brother well," Gentry said slowly, "but I usually do a little checking before we set up to do serious business with a store. I understand Larry never made a success of anything before. Could his business be floundering and someone is about to foreclose?"

Kandy set her glass of tea down and stared into it for a moment before she answered. "I don't think that's it. A few times he has shown me his week's receipts. They were outstanding for a store of this size. The biggest sales were on paintings by local artists. But what has bothered me is where he got the money to set up his gift shop." Why was she confiding in Gentry like this?

Gentry pushed back his plate and sipped his coffee. "Could your father have financed him."

"No way!" Kandy said emphatically. "Dad loaned Larry money for several ventures and they all were failures. He absolutely refused to loan him any more money."

"Larry didn't tell you where he got the money to start Blue Corn Treasures?"

Kandy grimaced, "I asked him but he was quite secretive about his benefactor. That has disturbed me. Could he have gotten the money from a criminal element that have their clutches into him and he can't get loose?"

"There's always that possibility but I hope it isn't that bad," Gentry said. "Maybe this evening I'll get a chance to talk with him. If he's in financial trouble maybe I can help. I believe in Larry. He's got a good business here and I don't want to see him fail."

"You would do that for Larry?" Kandy asked incredulously.

Gentry nodded his sandy head, "I wouldn't for everyone, of course, but I sense there is good stuff in Larry. He needs a chance and I believe his gift shop has real potential."

A short while later as they entered historical Bent Street, Kandy explained, "This street was named for Charles Bent who was

New Mexico's first appointed governor. A mob killed him on this street, enraged because the United States had annexed New Mexico after the Mexican War. Imagine, we are walking on ground where men actually spilled a governor's blood," Kandy said with a shudder.

"I'm afraid most of the soil of our fair country has drunk the blood of violence," Gentry said. "I don't live far from the Mexican border and murder — usually drug related — happens often in our border towns. It makes a person long for the time when God will put a stop to it all."

The remainder of the afternoon was spent visiting the wool shops, the myriad art galleries and craft shops, strolling together along the narrow streets, hand in hand.

Later, as they rested on a tree-shaded, picturesque bench on a broad paved corridor which ran between small shops, Gentry told Kandy about his family.

"My mother and dad were the housekeeper and gardener at Coppercrest, the Barfield mansion, and I grew up there. I lived in awe of Cyrus Barfield the owner of Gypsy Blue Enterprises. He was stern, despotic and not at all kind or lovable, but I was extremely grateful when he sent me to college. Not too long ago I discovered that

Cyrus was my father."

"My, that's straight out of a gothic novel!" Kandy exclaimed. She suddenly sobered, "How is your relationship with your natural father now?"

Gentry's laugh held a tinge of bitterness. "I've had a problem with the lordly master of Coppercrest mansion tossing my mother aside when he found she was to bear his son. I'm sure he pushed easy-going John Howard into marrying my mother Matilda. I still go by the name of the only father I ever knew."

"You said you have shares in the company. So your father finally did acknowledge you?"

"Yes, and he is trying to make it up to me in his own rough way. But Cyrus is not a lovable man — although he has come to know the Lord recently. He doesn't really know how to show affection. But he gave me my own nicely furnished apartment at Coppercrest, and shares in the company. I'm grateful to God for those things."

"Coppercrest sounds so gorgeous, I would love to see it."

Then she felt her face grow hot and dropped her eyes. What will he think of me, she thought. That I'm inviting myself for a visit to the home of a man I have only known for less than two days!

Gentry didn't seem to notice. His warm, vibrant voice was saying eagerly, "It would be my pleasure to show it to you sometime."

"You said your step-brother and his wife influenced you for God. I'd like to meet them." There I go again, she thought gloomily. Gentry will think I'm asking to meet his family!

"They would like you," Gentry said. She looked up to see Gentry watching her face intently and she flushed right up into the roots of her hair.

"You-you have the strangest way of looking at me," she stuttered, getting quickly to her feet.

Gentry stood up also and laid a gentle hand on her arm. "I'm sorry. I didn't mean to be rude but you have the most expressive face I ever saw. It is never the same, but changes from moment to moment as if your emotions and thoughts are mirrored there."

"I'm not sure I want anyone to read my thoughts and feelings!"

Gentry laughed, "I'm not a mind reader but I wouldn't mind being able to read yours." His voice now held a teasing note.

The day had been pure joy to Kandy and as they were driving toward The Lodge late that evening, Kandy could not recall when she had felt so comfortable — or so exhilarated — in anyone's company. She and Adria enjoyed each other's company but she found herself, selfishly she acknowledged, almost desperately hoping Adria would not want to accompany them tomorrow.

Adria is so pretty, she thought despairingly. I love her like a sister but I couldn't bear it if he starts noticing her instead of me! She found herself wishing faithless Giles would show up suddenly. She would have no problem with Adria, then!

But I could never compete favorably with lovely Adria for a man, she thought. Never!

But that night at dinner, all thoughts of competing with Adria for Gentry's attentions were quickly forgotten as Adria related the happenings of her day.

"Do you really think that was Giles whistling?" Kandy asked.

"I just don't know," Adria said. "But there is someone up there camping in the cave, with a whole arsenal of weapons!"

Sibyl laughed, "It's hardly an arsenal. Lots of people have guns. . . ."

"But why would a person want to camp out and carry along three guns and a wicked-looking knife?"

"This is a scary time to live in," Sibyl reasoned. "If I was camping out I would want a weapon."

"But three guns and a knife seems a little 'much' to me for a common camper. And that rifle had a scope on it. Besides, why is that man camping on posted Graham land?"

Again Sibyl answered, "It wouldn't be the first time we have had to evict trespassers. Our mountains are beautiful and some people ignore no-trespassing signs as if they weren't there."

"Perhaps I should go up in the morning and check-out this trespasser," Larry said. "I don't mind so much the man camping up there but I don't like the idea of his having guns — especially a high powered rifle — that close to our home. I can go up before I go to work in the morning."

"I'd like to go too, if you wouldn't mind," Gentry said. "I'd jump at an excuse to climb one of your mountains."

"You don't need an excuse," Larry said with a grin, "I'd like to have your company."

"Is it okay with you if we postpone our sightseeing," Gentry asked Kandy.

"That's fine with me," Kandy said.

"Why don't you and I tag along, Kandy?" Adria asked.

"Of course we're going," Kandy said with

a grin, "I wasn't about to let them go without us." She turned to Gentry, "The caves aren't spectacular as caves go but Larry, Adria and I have played in them all our lives."

"You three could go on up to the gazebo and have a picnic afterward," Larry said. "I wish I could go too but it's back to the salt-mine for this working stiff."

Kandy was relieved to see that Larry seemed almost like himself tonight, perhaps a little quiet, but not deeply depressed as he seemed earlier in the day. Maybe he really had been just feeling queasy. He had certainly put away his share of Sibyl's roast beef, potatoes and hot biscuits tonight!

"Why don't we take Sarge along?" she heard Adria saying. "I'm still puzzled at how Sarge acted when he heard that man whistling. He acted like he knew him well. And I'm almost certain he trailed the guy when I released him from the leash."

"Giles is the only one besides you, Kandy, that Sarge ever acted that foolish about," Larry said thoughtfully. "Remember we used to kid Giles that he was stealing your dog's love?"

"That's what has me so puzzled," Adria said. "But if that was Giles out there on the mountainside, why would he run away from me? It just doesn't make sense!"

Chapter 12

The next morning when the whole party visited the inner cave where Adria had found the camping equipment and guns the day before, the room was empty. Before they left the chamber every nook and cranny was searched but not even an empty can was found to show that anyone had ever camped there.

Finally satisfied that the unknown stranger had moved out, they headed out through the low passageway toward the exit. "At least we don't have to worry about that guy taking a pot-shot at one of us," Adria called back to the others.

As Larry, the last one, climbed out of the cave and clambered down to stand with the party on the trail below, Adria suddenly raised her hand and motioned for silence. For a brief time there was no sound except the chattering of a fluffy-tailed squirrel on a tree branch and the raucous squawk of a crow.

Then faintly to their straining ears came the warbling of bird-calls. The melodious trilling seemed to drift in on the breeze, floating down from the mist-shrouded mountaintop.

"Giles used to do bird-calls," Kandy whispered to Adria. "I used to love to hear them. He could entice birds right up to us, remember."

"I remember," Adria whispered back. "Now — listen to that. . . ." The bird-calls had ceased and strains of "I Dream of Jeannie" now wafted to their ears.

"That makes goose bumps on my arms," Kandy said softly. "If that isn't Giles whistling, I never heard him, and I did — many times."

Larry leaned over to whisper to Adria, "Do you recall how Giles used to change the words of that song to 'I Dream of Adria with the Light Brown Hair?' "

A lump swelled up into Adria's throat so she couldn't speak, but she nodded numbly.

"He could have been a singer — professionally — if he had chosen to be," Larry mused, forgetting to whisper. "Remember, he took music as a minor in college and he sang solos with a college group regularly."

Perhaps Larry's voice carried to the unseen whistler because the sound abruptly broke off and although they listened intently for several minutes, it did not resume.

"Whether that was your Giles fellow or not, apparently that was your mystery man heading out of your neck of the woods,"

Gentry said, "carrying his camping gear and guns with him."

After Larry went away to his work day in Taos, Adria, Kandy and Gentry climbed about the ruggedly beautiful mountain slopes for the remainder of the day. Although they visited the gazebo, they didn't lunch there. They found a small rocky creek bed with a tiny stream meandering through it and roasted wieners and marshmallows over a small, carefully-guarded fire under a rocky overhang.

As the day progressed in Gentry's company, Adria began to see what Kandy saw in the stranger who had landed in their midst. Gentry was a tall, powerfully built man but he was gentle and protective toward Kandy and herself. Although he wasn't handsome, she quickly sensed a sensitive, kind nature in the man. Intelligent and witty, he treated them both with an old fashioned courtesy that was refreshing. Yet, for all his evident gentleness, she recalled that Larry said Gentry was tough, though fair, in matters of business.

Adria saw his warm green-hazel eyes rest often on Kandy throughout the day and was glad. Had Kandy at last found someone who could usurp Sarge's place in Kandy's heart? Even as she felt her heart bound with happiness at the thought, Adria felt a deep sadness for herself. Her own heart seemed forever tied to Giles — a man who had jilted her! Yet she still loved him.

As she followed Gentry, Kandy, and Sarge homeward late that evening, Adria again thought of the whistling voice of the man out on the misty mountainside. He sounds so much like Giles, she thought, but common sense tells me he cannot be. Sudden tears rose into her eyes and she wiped them away angrily. Why could she never get away from the memory of Giles Hughlet! Wherever she turned there were reminders of him.

"Dear God," she prayed softly, again swiping at the wetness that brimmed in her eyes, "Some way let me find a peace about Giles. Either bring him back to me, or take him out of my heart for good. I want to live my life in the present, not in the past."

Later that evening Adria had just finished bathing and getting into a sea-green skirt with a matching green and white blouse when she heard Larry's cheerful call, "Anybody home?"

She went to her door and heard Sibyl answer from somewhere inside the house, "The girls are upstairs but I think I heard Gentry go into the family room."

"I hope you've fixed something for dinner that can keep," Larry called to Sibyl, "because I've made reservations at Doc Martin's in Taos Inn for this evening."

Adria heard the quick click of Sibyl's heels on the polished hardwood of the hallway and then her voice came plainly to Adria from just below the stairs. "That wasn't necessary, Larry," she remonstrated, "I have a perfectly lovely turkey in the oven."

"Don't worry your pretty little head about it, ma chère," Larry said, with an indulgent chuckle. "We've got company, let's live it up a little."

"But isn't Doc Martin's terribly expensive," Sibyl said worriedly.

"Not that much and besides, I'm doing well financially now, so a little splurge now and then doesn't hurt."

"W-well I suppose it won't be too bad with just you four."

"None of that 'just you four' bit," Larry scolded fondly. "You are going with us! It's time you got out of the house a little anyway."

"I really don't have the time," Sibyl said quickly. "I'm working on a new painting and while it's going well, I really should finish it. You know that I don't have a lot of time to devote to my painting now that Dad is incapacitated."

"Let the nurse take care of him," Larry said decisively. "That's what she's paid for!"

"But Dad will scarcely eat a bite if I don't feed him."

"How well I know it!" Larry said fiercely, "That old tyrant tied you to him so you never have dared have a life of your own!"

"Larry! That's your father you're talking about! Besides, the poor man is a cripple now."

"He never let you have a life of your own before he came down with this stroke!" Larry said bitterly. "It isn't fair! You're not his wife but he's made you take the place of one!"

"Someone had to take care of the house and of your father, Larry. He was a brilliant lawyer so he never had the time or capacity for dealing with a busy household," Sibyl said patiently.

"You are going with us, Sibyl," Larry declared. "Dad dozes a lot and he will never miss you."

"Well, I suppose it would be rather pleasant," Sibyl said.

Suddenly it came to Adria that she was listening in on a private conversation and she stepped back into her room and closed the door softly.

Sibyl! It had never occurred to Adria that the motherly woman would desire any life than her role here. And perhaps she was happy in her life here, in spite of Larry's angry accusations.

Did Sibyl have aspirations to be a selling artist? She knew that Sibyl puttered around with painting, had even taken classes and had her own private studio at the back of the house. She had heard Benjamin Graham refer to Sibyl's painting as "my eldest daughter's little hobby".

Adria sat down on the side of the bed and mused. Sibyl had seemed middle aged all the time Adria was growing up, yet she probably wasn't middle aged even now. Had Benjamin Graham selfishly tied his timid, submissive elder daughter to this house, denying her a life of her own? It was a new and disturbing thought.

But surely Sibyl loved her place in this home! Sibyl had always been at the center of the Graham family's life, baking, seeing to the cleaning, washing and shopping.

Sarah and Fritz had been housekeeper and all-around-handyman all of Adria's growing up years. But it was Sibyl who gave them their orders and kept the household running smoothly, many times working right beside one or the other of them.

With an odd twist in her heart, Adria suddenly realized that Sibyl was still a comparatively young woman. She recalled once that Larry had said she was only twelve when Benjamin had married Larry and Kandy's delicate mother Katherine. So she was only thirteen years older than Larry.

Adria walked to the window and looked out into the gathering dusk. The trees were bathed in a breath-taking wash of flaming orange-red. But tonight her heart did not bound up at the sight. What had it been like for Sibyl — rather plain and painfully shy around strangers — to have lovely Katherine for a stepmother?

Adria looked deep in her mind and realized that Katherine had never run this household. She was a lovely but delicate and sickly ornament that Benjamin had adored and lavished everything on that money could buy. He had taken time for her and even gave some quality time to Larry, and especially to Kandy, but she could never recall his showing any appreciation or affection for busy, bustling Sibyl.

Adria felt a pang go through her. Sibyl had been forced to take on her young shoulders the running of this household and after a while the care of two babies, born only two years apart. But in all her time of coming to The Lodge, Adria could never recall Sibyl complaining.

Maybe she didn't really mind, Adria thought. Some people are just cut out to be homemakers. Maybe being the axis around which The Lodge ran smoothly and efficiently was Sibyl's desire and not something foisted on her by a domineering father.

I hope so, Adria thought. Sibyl held a very special part in Adria's heart and it hurt to think she might have carried too heavy a load all these years, especially if it had been against her will.

Adria loved Uncle Benjamin, but the respected, forceful, articulate attorney could never have been considered lovable, except by Kandy, his youngest and obviously the favorite of his three children.

There was a tap at her door and Kandy pushed it open and announced that Larry was taking them to Doc Martin's for dinner.

"What's so special about Doc Martin's," Adria asked impishly.

"Don't act dumb girl! You know they serve some of the best food around Taos — and in real atmosphere. How does 'Filete al Chipotle' sound, or maybe you would rather have

114

'Pechugas de Pollo con Rajas', dear lady."

"Speak English and I might know if I have the nerve to try it. Food with foreign names, even Spanish, always leaves me with the horror that I might be eating roasted grasshoppers or sauteed earthworms with mushrooms."

"For the benefit of my ignorant cousin from the city, maybe chicken breasts baked with pablano chili strips, served with an ancho cream sauce, sounds better, and I know you would love the grilled beef tenderloin served on a blue corn tortilla with a chipotle chili sauce."

"They both sound Mexicany and you know I love anything Mexican so I'm game if you are. On my salary most of my dining out is done at McDonald's but I certainly don't mind living a little higher."

"Seriously, they do serve some wonderful food there in that historic old inn and a good variety," Kandy said. "And say, why don't you wear your straw sandals and your new skirt and blouse. With a bright scarf around your neck, you will look good enough to eat."

"You look pretty cute yourself," Adria said. And she did. Her dark hair was swept up on the top of her shapely head, and the warm red dress, with a full skirt belted to her slim waist by a braided leather belt, set off her smooth tanned skin. A wide, white lace collar with a small mother of pearl pin at the throat added a festive note.

"You should dress up more often," Adria said with a quick hug. Then with an exaggerated frown, she added teasingly, "But there's a danger there. If it happens too often I'll be losing you from our spinsterhood club."

"If it's to the right man, I might relinquish my membership to that exclusive club," Kandy said airily.

"Could the right man be sandy-haired and green eyed and be from Bisbee, Arizona?"

Suddenly the glow went out of Kandy's dark eyes and she dropped her head. When she looked up again her face was anguished. "Adria, I have never really cared greatly if I was attractive to men or not. My work and home life are satisfying, but all of that has changed since I met Gentry. What if he doesn't like me, I mean — really like me?"

"I don't think you need to worry about Gentry not liking you," Adria said. "I've seen his eyes on you all day."

Kandy's cheeks regained a little of their rich glow and she said tensely, "Well, he did ask me to be his date tonight and I know he thinks my face is interesting, he told me so, but. . . ."

"He'll think your face is more than just interesting tonight," Adria said confidently. "And how did he happen to say you had an interesting face? That's a strange thing to tell a girl."

"There's a little girl in a picture in Larry's shop that Gentry says has my face. It didn't do my ego much good for him to tell me she wasn't pretty — but was striking and interesting."

"Get that worry frown off your face and just be yourself," Adria said. "And then if your knight in shining armor doesn't like you then mark him off your list as a dumb male that isn't worth your time."

"I don't want to mark him off," Kandy said glumly. "Adria, you have gone out with lots of guys and I have been out with very few. Couldn't you give me a few pointers about what to say and how to act. Out sightseeing in a shirt and jeans is one thing but in a dress-up situation, I'm tongue-tied and clumsy."

"The best advice I could give you is just be yourself. You are a very attractive young lady and a person well worth knowing.

"Don't try to impress Gentry Howard. I have the feeling that he would see through that in a hurry. You have been with him almost constantly the past two days. You should know his interests and what you have in common. Just try to relax and have a good time."

Kandy looked sheepish, "Imagine me caring this much if any man likes me or not. This surely doesn't sound like the old take 'em or leave 'em forest ranger, does it?"

"It makes a difference when you suddenly begin to care, doesn't it," Adria said gravely. "I should know."

Chapter 13

Much later that night, Adria changed into cotton pajamas and drew a cool terry-cloth robe over them. Tonight had been such fun: relaxed conversation, lovely surroundings, delicious food. The roasted pheasant breast with a juniper berry demi-glace that she had chosen was out of this world. She had sampled Larry's grilled New Zealand venison, and Gentry's pepper crusted lamb loin, with butter flavored pasta. Both had been scrumptious. She sighed now with regret that she had been too replete to try one of the exotic sounding desserts.

She chuckled as she remembered Gentry's almost boyish delight that he had outmaneuvered Larry and paid the restaurant bill. After they had all ordered, Gentry had excused himself to make a telephone call. When Larry had asked for the bill at the end of the meal, the waitress had informed him it was already paid. Gentry had paid it when he went to make his call. When Larry had remonstrated with him, Gentry told him he was beginning to feel like a starboarder and paying the bill would repay them a little bit.

As Adria brushed her teeth her thoughts swung to Kandy. After her initial panic in Adria's room, she had carried off her part of the evening with poise and obvious enjoyment.

While not being aloof from the others, again Gentry had showed in little ways that he was greatly attracted to Kandy. With charming ease, he seated Kandy and saw to her comfort before anyone else. A rare glow had made Kandy's face almost beautiful all evening.

Sibyl had seemed a little uncomfortable at first but Larry — bless him — had not allowed her to feel out-of-pocket. It wasn't that Sibyl had never gone out socially or entertained. She had often been hostess at dinners when her father entertained clients and colleagues at The Lodge. And they had been asked to the homes of the elite of society in the area. But she recalled that Sibyl had never really seemed to enjoy these events. It was just part of the role she was called upon to play. And as everything else she did, she carried it off well.

Adria had always enjoyed the company of her handsome cousin Larry and he had been the life of the party that evening, joking and jovial. Kandy had confided to her that Larry had seemed greatly troubled that morning but whatever problem had rested so heavily upon him that morning must have been resolved.

She grimaced as she recalled one little incident of the evening that she felt might have been embarrassing for Larry. The maitre d' brought them a wine list. Larry had seemed amazed when Gentry told him that he never drank anything stronger than Coke. Sibyl didn't drink and neither Kandy nor Adria had since they became Christians. So Larry also refused an alcoholic beverage — to Adria's relief, because sometimes Larry drank a little too much and got decidedly silly.

After brushing and flossing her teeth, Adria washed and creamed her face, noting with satisfaction that her cheeks seemed to have taken on a healthier glow with just a couple of days in the mountain air.

She switched off the light, opened the French doors and stepped onto the small balcony which she shared with Kandy in the next room. She had rather hoped Kandy would want to sit up and talk but after only a few minutes of chatting in Adria's room, Kandy had said she was tired and had departed.

Kandy had told her earlier in the day about her brief encounter with her attacker.

But if it was bothering Kandy tonight she had certainly showed no signs. Idly she wondered if the man really was the one who had attacked her cousin. Obviously Larry did not think so. Kandy said that Larry vaguely knew the man and had scoffed at her assertion that the bearded man was the culprit.

There was no way of proving it on the man if it were true, it would just be her word against his. It was an alarming thought that the sadist was still out there, free to beat another victim at will.

Adria crossed to lean upon the parapet that surrounded the balcony and stared out into the night. Some clouds drifted here and there and a slight breeze brushed her cheeks. She could hear the occasional sleepy twittering of birds in a huge tree not far from the house. A lone call of a coyote quavered out in the woods and after a moment there came an answering call from nearer the house.

Below, Adria heard a low growl from Sarge and smiled. He had a comfortable doghouse below, under Kandy's window, but seldom slept in it. He prowled the fenced-in grounds around the house during the night and did a lot of his sleeping during the day.

A silvery moon slid from behind a gray shred of cloud and lit up much of the yard, but her balcony lay in shadows. She thought she saw something move between the trunks of two large trees that crowded the edge of the lawn. Then she saw Sarge walking stiff-legged and menacing across the grass toward the now-stilled movement. I hope it isn't a porcupine, she thought. Adria was on the point of calling him back when she heard his low whine.

Adria squinted her eyes and stared at the shadowy spot where Sarge now stood. Was that a whisper she heard? She wasn't sure but as she continued to stare, holding her breath in order to hear better, she vaguely saw a figure move just at the edge of the trees. The moonlight did not reach under the trees but she thought it might be the outline of a man. Surely not, she thought incredulously.

Sarge seemed to be rubbing his head against something. There was more movement but it was hard to see what was going on in the deep, dappled shadows. A figure stepped closer to the edge of the shadow and she was almost certain it was a human form. Was it squatting down? She could hear Sarge's whimper of pleasure. Was someone scratching the dog's head and ears?

Then the figure stood up and stepped a little farther out of the shadows and lifted his head to stare up toward the balcony where she stood. Shock slammed into her body like a battering ram. For now she could see the figure was tall, very thin, with an old hat pulled down over his head. The man was her admirer who dogged her steps around Albuquerque!

Anger washed over her in waves. How dare he follow her to Taos! Then a new thought came: how had he found her? For a moment she almost screamed at him and then she remembered that she might wake Kandy and the rest of the household.

What did the man want with her? Protecting her was one thing but following her about and spying on her every move was infuriating! She was too angry now to be afraid of the stranger.

Stealthily she slid back inside and softly closed the door. Dashing through halls and down stairs on bare feet, within minutes she was at the back door. Sliding back the bolt, she eased out the door.

All was quiet. She glanced up at the side of the building to locate the balcony that opened off her room. The place where the man had stood a few minutes before should be a little to her left but clearly visible from where she stood. But nothing moved at the edge of the trees.

Softly she moved down the steps of the side stoop and walked out onto the wide stone sidewalk. For a moment she stood there and then started determinedly toward where the man must have stood. Perhaps he had gone back into the deep shadows under the trees but he couldn't get off the grounds on this side because of the high fence that surrounded the yard.

Fear shivered down her neck, but she thrust it aside angrily. She was sick and tired of this man following her around and she planned to tell him so — and that she was going to take drastic steps if he persisted! Stopping at the edge of the shadows, she peered into the dimness under the trees. There were no bushes or flowers under these trees and the fence was just beyond them.

Nothing stirred there. Even Sarge seemed to have vanished. A trickle of fear quivered over her but resolutely she stepped under the shadowy depth of the trees. Now she could see clearly. There was no one here. Where had the intruder gone, how could he have gotten out?

Suddenly something cold and wet touched her hand and she jumped violently and shrieked. Jerking quickly around, she saw that it was Sarge. His tongue was hanging out as if he were grinning and she could see the glint of his eyes. She put her hand on his head and stroked him, trying to still her rapidly beating heart. Scanning the grounds with her eyes, she saw no one; in fact, nothing moved except for the slight swaying of a branch above her head, stirred by a sudden burst of breeze.

Surely she couldn't have imagined there was a man out here! Yet, how could he have gotten to the back or front gates so quickly. Of course if he had seen her on the balcony then he could have gotten out easily in time.

But Sarge would never have allowed a stranger to come into the yard. Except the man who had been camped out in the cave and could whistle just like Giles! Of course! That was who it was. Not the stranger who followed her around Albuquerque, but the whistler! Relief melted the strength from her limbs and she sank down on the pine needles. In spite of the fact that the whistler from the misty hillside apparently had guns in his gear, she wasn't as frightened of him as of the unknown man who followed her around Albuquerque.

Sarge tried to climb in her lap and she gently shoved him off. He contented himself with laying his head against her shoulder.

"I wonder how that stranger out there won you over so completely," Adria murmured against his fur. "And what was the man doing inside our private yard? Just when we thought he was gone, here he is back — and right in our own yard in the dead of night."

She must tell Larry and Fritz about this. The man might be a burglar. Hadn't she read in the paper that there was a burglary recently in a mansion and an extremely expensive painting was taken? No — now she recalled, the painting had been found later in another part of the house where apparently a servant had rehung it. But just the same this stranger must not be allowed to roam about the grounds at will.

She went slowly back across the grass to the house, bade Sarge good night, and returned quietly to her room. But for a long time she was unable to sleep. Twice she thought she heard a strange noise outside and slipped out onto the balcony to investigate. Once it had been Sarge patrolling the grounds and the other time she could see nothing amiss. She resolved to tell Larry about their night-time visitor.

But the next morning Adria told no one about the prowler. Sometime during the night she had come up with a plan of her own and she could scarcely wait until the others were gone to put it into operation. She was going to find the camping place of the whistler and talk to him whether he wanted to talk to her or not!

Her plan was simple. Sarge obviously knew the man and had searched him out two days before. If he did that today, all she had to do was follow him to the mystery man! A little prickle of fear ran down her backbone but she shrugged it off. There might be a slight element of danger — since the man had weapons — but he had simply slipped away the other day when she had called to him so he wasn't trying to harm any of them. Besides, with Sarge along as her protector she needn't worry.

Gentry and Kandy had invited her to go with them today on an all-day trip to Taos Indian Pueblo and the old historic Martinez home.

"Thanks for the offer," she had said, "but I'm enjoying just being outside in the woods. I plan to take a book along and make a day of it if I can borrow Sarge again."

After the others were gone, Adria found that Sibyl had already packed her a lunch. "I'm not sure it's a good idea for you to go up on the mountain alone," Sibyl said.

"After all, we don't know if that man who was camped in the cave has really gone."

Adria almost told her about the prowler of the night before but decided against it. She would make so much fuss that Adria would be forced to spend her day close to the house. "Sarge will protect me," she told Sibyl with a quick hug.

"I still don't like you going out there alone; remember what happened to Kandy out in the forest," Sibyl finished darkly.

Unease slid its cold knife into Adria's inner being, and for a moment she wondered if she was being wise to go out searching for the mystery man, or even if she should go alone so far into the woods. Then she thrust it away. As a reporter in Albuquerque, a city known for its high crime rate, she traveled alone all the time to gather her news stories.

"I'll be careful," she reassured her concerned cousin.

With a final quick wave she went out the back door. An exhilarating sense of adventure washed over her as if she were on the trail of a thrilling news story. Would she find the whistler? If she did, what kind of man would he be? With his whistling ability, she couldn't imagine that he could be anything evil.

What if it turned out to be Giles, after all? She shut that thought from her mind. Why ruin her day with thoughts of the man who had jilted her? She should take the advice she gave Kandy about Gentry. If Giles doesn't care for me, why don't I realize he's not worth mooning over.

Chapter 14

Clouds still obscured the top slopes of the mountains as Adria and Sarge went out the back gate. She waved to Sarah and Fritz who were working in the large family vegetable garden. Fritz was using an old-fashioned hand plow to turn over the rich dark soil between rows of green onions and curly lettuce. She recalled that her uncle had offered to buy Fritz a garden tiller or garden tractor but he had scorned such a concession to modern gardening. Sarah was gathering green beans into a large kettle.

Adria left Sarge on a leash until they reached the cave, then released him with an order to stay with her. Mist swirled about them as they climbed slowly higher on the trail but they could see the trail for a short way ahead most of the time. At first Sarge kept looking back for more instructions but when she gave none he stopped looking back and began trotting a little faster. Twice she had to call to him to slow down.

"I hope you know where you're going," she muttered. Sarge had left the trail and was circling large boulders, moving downhill into gullies, and then uphill until she was completely lost. Now they were crossing — at a sharp upward slant — a stretch of mountainside so full of brush between trees of every size that they could scarcely push through.

"Let's rest, Sarge," she said. Every breath hurt, she was panting so hard in the damp cool air. She looked up and realized that Sarge was no longer with her. "Oh, great!" she mumbled to herself. "Get yourself lost, Adria, with your big adventure!"

For several minutes she sat still, too winded to attempt to climb further. She called Sarge once, but only softly. Surely he would come back for her when he realized she was no longer following him, and she didn't want to scare the whistler away if his camp was near.

She lay back as well as she could against a prickly bush and closed her eyes. "I'm sure getting out of shape," she said softly to herself. "It's about time I did some strenuous climbing."

She struggled out of her small pack and took off her sweater then promptly put it back on. Her shirt was damp with perspiration and the misty air stuck the cold cloth to her warm body, causing her to shiver.

"I sure don't want to get a summer cold," she muttered to herself.

After a moment she noticed the air was full of the hum of bees and insects buzzing about blossoms on some of the bushes. A pine cone fell near her and she looked up to see a perky jay staring down at her. Peering ahead through an opening in the brush and trees she saw what appeared to be a little clearing. Getting tiredly to her feet, she picked up her pack and pushed through the brush. When she emerged, she gasped in wonder. The clearing was a pocket tucked into the woods, and grass and wild flowers of many hues carpeted the ground. She gazed in wonder. How had she missed this enchanting place in her ramblings. The murmur of water trickling over pebbles and rocks, and the singing and chirping of birds fell pleasantly on her delighted ears. For several moments she stood there, drinking in the beauty of the place, before she saw the tent.

It was tiny, no more than six by eight, and was a shade of green that blended so perfectly with the grass that she almost didn't see it at all.

The flap was closed so she couldn't see into the interior. Her heart began to pound as her eyes carefully searched the little clearing. When she saw no one there, she cat-footed across the grass toward the tent.

As she approached it, she saw it sat back just a few feet from the rocky, sandy lip of a tiny stream. Rocks had been piled together to make a fireplace and a coffee pot sat over glowing coals. A frying pan — filled with bacon — rested on a large flat rock to the side.

Suddenly she realized the bacon was uncooked. She must have interrupted the camper's breakfast preparations. The hair on the back of her head prickled. Where was the camper? Swinging around she saw a tall thin man standing to her left under the trees. His long slim fingers rested lightly on Sarge's head.

Adria was starting to stammer out a greeting when the man spoke. "Good morning, ma'am. Is this your dog?" The voice was startlingly deep for such a thin man, with a pleasant huskiness about it.

"I'm sorry if I have intruded on your camp," Adria said apologetically. "You were making your breakfast. Please, don't let me interrupt you."

The stranger stood silently staring at her. She couldn't see his eyes as they were covered with dark sun glasses. Her reporter eyes quickly noted that his long frame was encased in clean but faded blue jeans and a denim jacket covered a black and red checked flannel shirt, opened at the neck. Over dark curling hair rested a worn felt hat.

When the man continued to gaze at her, Adria felt her face grow uncomfortably warm. But suddenly Sarge rescued her. He left the man and trotted to her side, rubbing his head on her jeans covered leg. Looking down at him, Adria found her tongue. "No, he belongs to my cousin Kandy Graham."

For the first time the man moved, with easy grace like a man used to being outdoors. He walked to the fire and bent down to set the frying pan over the glowing coals. "I have plenty of food, will you join me for breakfast?"

"Thank you, but no," Adria said. Her heart had now somewhat slowed its galloping and she felt more at ease. "I've had my breakfast long ago."

"I'm not much like the ordinary camper, I guess," the stranger said. "Even up here in the mountains I read late and sleep-in much of the time." He reached inside a wooden box Adria hadn't noticed before and took out a metal cup. "You will have some coffee, I hope."

"Yes, thank you, that smells delicious," Adria said, sitting on a camp-stool and accepting the cup gingerly, as he warned her it might be hot. It was, so she set it down quickly and poured in powdered cream and sugar that he passed her. He handed her a spoon and she stirred the steaming dark liquid that looked strong enough to dissolve metal.

The stranger folded his long body into a crouch, balanced on the balls of his feet and turned the bacon with a fork. His boots were scuffed and worn but recently polished, she noticed.

Laying the fork down, he shifted to face her, "I'm sorry, I forgot to introduce myself. I'm Sam Tillet and I'm afraid I'm trespassing on your land."

"My uncle's land," Adria corrected. "I'm Adria Graham and I'm just visiting from Albuquerque."

"Oh, from the big city." The tall man's husky voice was pleasant on the ear, Adria decided.

"And what do you do down there — if you will permit me to be so inquisitive?"

"I'm a newspaper reporter. What do you do, Mr. Tillet?"

"Call me Sam, I don't like anyone to call me mister." The stranger chuckled suddenly, a soft husky burst of sound. " 'Mister' makes me feel old."

Adria sipped the scalding coffee and found it good, if a bit strong for her taste.

She noticed Sarge nosing about in the trees at the edge of the woods, seeming content to remain in the clearing.

Sam turned to flip the bacon over again before he said slowly, "As to what I do, I'm writing a book. Or maybe I should say, I'm trying to write a book."

"What kind of book are you writing," Adria asked, and realized she was truly interested.

The man swung to face her again and Adria felt annoyance spring up inside her. Why didn't the guy take off those dark glasses so she could see his eyes. She always liked to see the expression in a person's eyes when she talked to him. One could usually learn much there. Those dark glasses made her feel like she was talking to a blank wall.

"Well," Sam was saying, "I'm a bit of an artist so I'm attempting a guidebook for this area, for nature-lovers. I'm drawing little sketches of the flowers, shrubs, trees and even a few of the lesser known animal life."

"That sounds fascinating, would you mind if I saw some of your drawings."

Sam turned away to transfer the crisp brown bacon to a metal plate, then broke two eggs into the skillet. He spoke with his back turned to her, apologetically, "I doubt that they are very good. To a professional writer, I'm afraid my poor efforts may seem extremely amateurish."

"Nonsense," Adria said, "I'm the amateur when it comes to drawing anything."

"Well, if you promise not to be too critical of my scribblings. I'm not sure my ego can take any until it gets hardened to the cruel world of the publishing field. . . ."

"I won't be — I promise!" Adria said quickly.

He had turned about and was watching her intently. She turned her head away. It was embarrassing to be stared at. Suddenly her eyes lit on the eggs sizzling in the pan and she said quickly, taking up a pancake turner that Sam had laid on the flat rock, "Why don't you let me watch your eggs while you get the drawings. I can look at them while you eat."

Abruptly, without saying a word, he stood to his tall height in one fluid motion and moved toward the tent. He paused when she asked him how he wanted them and said, "Over easy." Unzipping the entrance flap, he tied it back and stooped to slip inside.

As she tended the eggs, her thoughts were busy. The man was not Giles, but his voice did resemble Giles's voice. This man's was deeper with that huskiness that made it so pleasant. She felt a keen disappointment that the man wasn't Giles but was surprised that his voice stirred a flutter to her heart like nothing had done in a long while. Perhaps because it sounds a little like Giles', she thought.

As Adria sipped her coffee and studied the penciled drawings — while Sam ate his breakfast in silence — Adria was amazed at how lifelike they were. He had used colored pencils and she felt she could almost smell the scent of some of them.

"That's one of my favorites," Sam said suddenly, leaning toward her.

She glanced at his clean-shaven, rather bony face and saw a long scar near his square chin and high on the bronzed cheekbone was another. Both were faint but unmistakable when the sun illuminated his face. The thought flashed through her mind that perhaps the man had been in a serious accident and the covering dark glasses might be hiding a marring deformity.

"It's Fairy Slipper, or Calypso, and it grows in high elevations of 8500 up to about 11,000 feet. I never pick them," he went on, "as they are very fragile and even their roots can be destroyed or damaged by careless hands or feet."

"I know this one," Adria exclaimed. "It's a Columbine!"

"Well now," Sam said in a pleased voice. "I must be improving if you can recognize a bloom."

"I'm not very knowledgeable about wild flowers," admitted Adria. She moved to another drawing and said excitedly, "I know this one too — Indian Paintbrush!"

Sam had finished his meal and now set the plate down and leaned over to point to the next drawing. "I imagine you know that one too — Nelson Larkspur — it's very poisonous to cattle."

After the flowers there were sketches of a few small animals and birds but they weren't as expertly drawn as the flowers.

Looking up from the sketches, Adria asked casually, "Did you camp in the cave over closer to The Lodge before you moved here?"

If Sam's surprised reaction wasn't real he was a good actor. "No, I set my tent up here three or four days ago and this is the only place I have been. Why?"

Adria stared into the darkness of the irritating glasses and again wished the man would take off the shades so she could see his expression. "I found some camping equipment there and presumed the man I heard doing bird-calls, and whistling 'I Dream of Jeannie' was the one camping there. You are the whistler, aren't you?"

For a moment the man said nothing and then he laughed, a short bark that some way didn't sound mirthful, "So — I have been discovered! I hope I didn't disturb you with my warblings.

"I'm sorry that I wandered so close to The Lodge. I'm just a curious guy, I guess, and I wanted to see what that splendid old lodge looked like, close up. I was sitting on a rock resting, on my way back from looking it over, and started to whistle. I've always whistled, ever since I was a kid. Suddenly I heard someone calling a name — Giles, I think — and I realized I was about to be found trespassing." He chuckled. "So I hustled out of there mighty quick."

"You sounded so much like a friend of mine that I thought it was him."

"Giles?"

"Yes, Giles Hughlet."

The man was studying her face again in that intent, disconcerting way now so she turned away to watch Sarge cavorting in the grass in happy abandonment. Not wishing to discuss Giles with this stranger, she asked abruptly, "How did you make friends with Sarge?"

"Sarge? Oh, you mean the German Shepherd. I don't know — I've always liked dogs and I guess they know it." Was the answer too pat, too casual?

"You took a chance with Sarge. He's trained to attack on command."

"He is?" The astonishment seemed genuine. "I never would have guessed. I made friends with him months ago when I was up in this area doing sketches. One day he just showed up nearby. I spoke to him and he seemed a little leery at first but after a while he came over and lay down near me. I offered him a bit of sandwich I had in my pack. He didn't take it then but it wasn't long until he was sniffing me over. He seemed to decide I would do then, and not only ate the bite but started rubbing against me, wanting to have his ears scratched."

"I didn't know Kandy ever allowed Sarge to go out of the yard unless he was with someone he knew," Adria said quietly.

"I wondered about that too," Sam said easily. "He was obviously a valuable dog. Of course it only happened once until this past Monday when he must have followed me up, by scent, I guess — after you caught me near the cave and I took off."

"Then you know where the cave is?"

For a long moment Sam studied her and then said offhandedly, "I presume it must be near that big rock where I was sitting when you heard me whistling."

Suddenly he said seriously, "Say, am I about to be evicted from my camping space? I know I'm trespassing but I've been very careful to not trash up the place. If I could have a few more days I would have all the drawings I need."

"Why did you come into our yard late last night?"

Sam stood suddenly to his feet and Adria — suddenly wary of the man — did the same. Sarge came quickly and stood looking up into the face of the man and whined. Sam knelt and putting his hand under Sarge's chin, lifted it and spoke softly. "Old man you got me into trouble." Sarge barked sharply and wagged his tail.

Sam stood to his feet, "I'm sorry, I hope I didn't frighten you. All the lights were out so I didn't think anyone would see me."

He bent to scratch Sarge's ears and went on, "You see, I went into town yesterday and I saw this huge meaty bone at the market so I bought it for him. It was late when I got back but I have a strong flashlight — and as I said I'm a night-owl, so I brought it down to Sarge."

"That was a risky thing to do," Adria said sharply. "Someone could have shot you for a burglar."

"I know it was a stupid thing to do but I was lonely. When I got there and called softly, Sarge didn't come right away, so I slipped in the back gate and along the line of trees by the fence toward where I saw the other day that he had a doghouse. When Sarge heard me he growled but I whispered to him and he recognized me."

That is a phony story if ever I heard one, Adria was thinking and her incredulity must have shown plainly on her face because Sam chuckled and said plaintively, "I know it isn't a likely story but it's true, nevertheless."

For a moment Adria looked at him, trying to read his expression but again the annoying dark glasses defeated her. "All of us are concerned about the person who was camping in the cave because I saw three guns and a vicious-looking knife among his gear."

"Those I don't have. And I didn't camp in the cave, I swear!"

When Adria said nothing, Sam suddenly reached over and touched her on the arm. "Go in the tent and look over my stuff. You'll find no guns except an ancient .22 pistol that I slip on my belt when I'm climbing in rocks where rattlesnakes might be hiding."

When she made no move toward the tent, he stepped to the door and lifted the screen, "Go on, look inside."

"That's okay," she said slowly. "I believe you." And strangely she did.

"I insist."

So Adria reluctantly walked to the opening and glanced in.

"Go on in, I want you to be satisfied." So she did, stepping in hesitantly. He stayed outside as she gazed about the neat, well-arranged interior. At once she saw that the sleeping bag was dark-green and well-used, instead of new and bright blue.

There was a camp stove and a canvas bag, which probably held clothes, near one wall. A small portable typewriter rested on a card-table, a lawn chair sat nearby. An old pair of binoculars lay on the table as well as several books, colored pencils, a drawing pad, and other odds and ends a writer might need.

"Raise up the sleeping bag and see that I'm not hiding that cache of weapons you spoke of," Sam said. Was his tone slightly mocking? She complied but she had seen in the first glance that nothing here was new, not even the canteen that lay on a canvas camp stool.

Quickly Adria moved to the door and

Sam stepped back to allow her to exit. "I really did believe you," Adria said, "but you've made your point. Nothing is the same as I saw in the cave and there are no guns here."

"Except my trusty old .22, and it's there in my chuck box," Sam said, pointing. She saw it laying in a worn holster among some boxes and cans of food items.

"I really must go and let you get to your work," Adria said. "Thanks for the coffee."

Sam assured her she was not bothering him and seemed reluctant for her to leave which she observed with a quick lift of her heart. He followed her to the little stream and as she started away, he spoke again, "The old gentleman, your uncle, I heard in town that he has had a serious illness. How is he doing?"

Adria turned back, suddenly realizing that she also was wanting an excuse to stay longer. She told him briefly about the old man's serious condition. "It hurts us to see him so helpless, not even able to speak coherently. And he has always been so forceful, strong and articulate."

"I'm very sorry," the man said gently. "Your cousin, Kandy, I think you called her, I've seen her around. She wears the uniform of a forest ranger, I noticed. It must be terrible for her to see her father this way."

Adria idly saw that Sarge was digging vigorously at a hole near the tiny stream. "Yes, it has been terrible for her but Kandy can usually take everything in stride." She smiled, "I admire that in her, I'm afraid I don't do as well."

She looked up at the tall figure standing near her, "The last two years have been traumatic for Kandy. She lost her mother and shortly after was attacked by a hoodlum on a forest road and beaten severely. Then about six months ago her father suffered this incapacitating stroke."

Adria wished she could see his eyes as he said gently, "I'm so sorry. That's a lot of trouble in a short while. She must be a very strong young woman."

"God helps her," Adria said. "When she had about all she could take, shortly after that sadist attacked her, she met Jesus Christ and He has helped her tremendously. When I was going through a traumatic time, she introduced me to Jesus. God helped me as well." Adria felt a slight embarrassment at mentioning her new-found faith to this stranger but it seemed to come completely unbidden.

Sam said nothing for a brief interval but Adria immediately sensed a subtle change in demeanor, a slight stiffening of his lean frame, a tightening of his jaw, and balling of his long slim fingers. But she wasn't prepared for the deep bitterness that grated forth when he drew in a deep breath and spoke in a tight, curt, cutting voice.

"Where was this Jesus person when the man was beating your cousin? And where was he when your strong, articulate uncle became — in a snap of your god's fingers — a shriveled, helpless shell of a man!"

Shocked at his vehement and caustic words, Adria was for a moment at a complete loss for words. The man stood waiting as if daring her to refute his accusations.

"I-I never thought of it that way." She realized she was stuttering, but then she felt a flash of anger at his audacity in speaking against God and that steadied her.

Praying for help and guidance, she remained silent for a moment and then said quietly, "If God jumped in and stopped every tragedy and every accident, and never permitted us to feel pain or sorrow, how would we ever grow?"

Sudden deep pain edged Sam's voice as he said in a brittle, taut voice, "When He allows men who are monsters to abuse and kill helpless babies and children and torment and kill good, honest men and women, where is God in that! If there is a God! And if there is, he must be a monster himself to not put a stop to all the pain and suffering of this world!"

Adria stepped closer to Sam and touched his arm with a gentle hand. Her words were spoken softly, "Some horrible thing must have happened in your life to leave you so bitter and angry at God. I don't have all the answers but I do know that all the pain and suffering of this world came about as the result of the sin of the first woman and man."

"Why should others suffer for one couple's sins?" Sam grated through tightly compressed lips.

"The enemy of all God's creation won a great victory the day sin was committed. He is the one who controls the lives of those who wrack horror in this mad crazy world we live in," she reasoned.

"But if God is all powerful . . . ?"

"I do not presume to understand it all myself," Adria said, "but one thing I do know is that in the midst of any kind of trouble or heartache or pain, God will come to the individual who trusts him, and will give strength, comfort and even joy."

For a brief poignant moment Sam stood stiffly and then suddenly he took a deep breath and said curtly, "You better be careful wandering around in the forest. I saw a stranger not far from The Lodge yesterday. Goodbye ma'am."

Sam swung away from her, crossed to his tent and disappeared inside.

Chapter 15

For the next several days, Adria saw nothing of Sam Tillet. But her thoughts went often to him and his extreme bitterness and censure of God. It troubled her because she had sensed a deep and tearing pain behind his harsh words. Had the man lost a loved one in an accident or illness for which Sam was blaming God? Or had he seen some horrible atrocity — perhaps in war — that left frightful scars on his mind and emotions?

She wished she knew because in her one time encounter with Sam Tillet she had found someone she felt she would like to know better. What was there about the man that drew her? She could put her finger on nothing. What she could see of his face was not handsome, and his whip-lean physique was far too thin to be attractive. His voice was very pleasant but that seemed his only allurement.

But although she still rambled widely in the forest, and admitted to herself she was going out of her way to make a meeting with him happen, she saw not a glimpse of Sam. She carefully avoided going back to his camp, although she had cataloged landmarks in her memory so she could return if she desired. She didn't want the man to think she was running after him.

Growing tired of her own company, Adria went out with Gentry and Kandy several times. One day they drove to an all day Indian dance, another day they drove to Santa Fe to see the sights. One afternoon they took a hay-ride tour out to the Taos Pueblo that ended in a delicious chuck-wagon dinner in the hills, with guitar-picking singers and a cowboy poet for entertainment.

When Saturday came, Adria declined to go with Kandy and Gentry even though they graciously invited her. It was obvious to the most casual observer by now that Kandy and Gentry were deeply attracted to each other. Kandy's eyes were two bright stars these days and every time Gentry looked at Kandy, his whole face lit up. Adria decided she must not intrude on them again today.

So taking Sarge and a book she climbed to the gazebo and tried to settle down but for the first time in her life when she was at The Lodge, she felt discontent nagging at her. She was thrilled that Kandy had found someone to truly care for but she — Adria, the roving reporter — was still at loose-ends in her life. Giles had jilted her and obviously wasn't coming back, and even this new, interesting stranger had shown no inclination to get to know her.

And if he did, she told herself reluctantly, the man was not a Christian and it would never do for her to become too interested in him. Her heart warned her it would not be wise to marry a non-Christian.

As she lay on the lounge trying to keep her mind on the mystery story she was trying to read, a disturbing thought probed a cold finger into her heart. Was she to always be alone? She had no immediate family and Kandy would likely soon be in a home of her own with a full life. What is going to happen to me, she wondered morosely.

She laid the book down and stared up at the ceiling beams of the open-sided shelter. Even the thought of her newspaper work which had always brought her much satisfaction no longer brought joy to her heart. Was she jealous of Kandy's happiness? No, it wasn't that. But perhaps it did lead to her feeling of aloneness. She and Kandy had always been so close — and such dear friends. If Gentry and Kandy were to marry, would it ever be the same between Kandy and herself?

I think I'll go home tomorrow, she thought gloomily. Gentry had decided to spend his whole two weeks vacation in Taos and it would probably be better if she went back home so they wouldn't feel they had to ask her to accompany them when they no doubt would rather be alone. Yes, she would go home and get back on the job. The decision didn't bring a bound to her heart as it usually did when she had been away from her job, but being here at The Lodge was not doing her any good now.

Suddenly she heard Sarge's sharp delighted bark and sat up quickly. Leaning casually against the trunk of the huge pine tree not ten feet away stood Sam Tillet. She wondered how long he had been standing there watching her. Her hand nervously went to her hair to push the light brown tendrils back from her face. Why did her heart miss a beat and then pound so maddeningly?

Sarge charged over to him but for a moment Sam stood looking at her, ignoring the dog. His thin lips were unsmiling and even looked a little grim, she thought. His eyes were still covered with the large dark glasses. Then Sam's long thin fingers reached out to stroke the dog's head and his lips curved into a faint smile.

"Good morning," Sam said formally.

Adria answered just as formally and rose

to her feet. "Come on up," she invited.

Sam moved with easy grace to the steps and put his hand on the guard rail and looked up at her. "I was on my way up yonder," he waved a hand up toward the mountain top, "and I saw you lying here."

The whistler climbed the three steps and stepped out on the floor. He is so tall, she thought irrelevantly. "Sit down," she invited, motioning toward a wooden lawn chair.

But he made no move to do so. For a moment, he seemed to hesitate and then he spoke abruptly, "What I really came by for is to apologize. I was rude the other day when you spoke about your god, and I'm sorry. I had no right to ridicule your beliefs and I apologize."

Adria looked up at him and said simply, "I accept your apology." Then her voice softened and she said gently, "What really bothered me was how bitter and angry you are at God. You must have gone through an extremely painful experience to feel the way you do."

Sarge had climbed the steps behind Sam and now he stuck his nose in the man's hand and whined. Sam reached down to rub the dog's head before he said tonelessly, "I have been but I didn't have to take it out on you."

"Would you like to talk about it?" Adria was surprised at her boldness.

His lips again curved into a cynical half-smile, "Thanks, but no. It's not a nice story."

"I'm a newspaper writer so I've heard a lot of not so nice stories."

"I'm sure you have but this is one I never tell anyone."

"Sometimes it helps to talk to someone," Adria said.

Sam's lips twisted as if with pain and he turned away. "It wouldn't help me, or you either, to tell this story. It's one I never can escape, and believe me I've tried."

He started down the steps and Adria knew suddenly that she didn't want this man to leave. Not yet!

Sam was now stepping off the treads to the rocky ground and she said quickly, "How are you coming with your book?" She moved down to the second step.

He turned back and grinned, more natural now, "Today I'm going up to see if I can find anything that I don't have in my collection. I hope to be finished and moving out by tomorrow."

"Where do you live?"

For a long moment it appeared that he wasn't going to answer, then he said casually, "In the Albuquerque area."

Suddenly an idea came to Adria and she said slowly, "I remember a flower that I didn't see in your collection. Maybe you have it now but if you don't, I remember where I saw several."

"What does it look like?"

"It's called Little Red Elephant. Kandy told me the name."

"Sure — also known as Lousewort. Has little elephant-like trunks. I've heard it can be used as a mild relaxant. That's one I forgot."

"I'll be glad to show you where there are some blooms," Adria offered.

"I shouldn't take up your time," Sam protested.

Adria laughed lightly, "I'm a little bored today anyway, so I'm glad to have something to do."

"Well — if you're sure," Sam said.

The day was pure delight as far as Adria was concerned but she wondered sometimes if Sam was having a good time. He was such a strange man. It was almost as if he let himself go sometimes and for a short while he would talk lightheartedly. Then he would lapse into a brooding silence and not talk for a long while, answering her lighthearted chatter with as few words as pos-

157

sible. She sensed a deep pain — like an unhealed grievous wound in his spirit. What had happened to this man that tore him apart, she wondered.

Adria had climbed to the place where the flowers were only once before and it was a rough climb, quite high on the mountain. Sarge never seemed to tire but Adria had to rest as they clambered around and over boulders and struggled through thick brush. But finally she found the wildflowers and Sam's delighted reaction was worth all the effort.

Before Sam sketched the flowers, they shared their lunch. Adria had brought some fried chicken, home-made rolls, green olives, doughnuts and milk. Sam brought out flour tortillas wrapped around chopped beef roast and some delicious picante sauce. When he produced two large red apples, Adria wondered if he had planned to share his lunch with her. There was obviously too much for one. Adria had packed extra in case she ran into Sam.

"I cooked the roast in a metal bucket in a pit lined with hot coals while I was gone yesterday," Sam said. "But the tortillas and sauce I bought from a Mexican friend."

A slight quiver ran over Adria and she said quickly, "The only one I ever knew who cooked things in a bucket like that was the friend I spoke of, Giles Hughlet. He always enjoyed camping."

Sam spoke carelessly, "What happened to this Giles fellow? Is he still around?"

"I really don't know," Adria said candidly. "We were engaged to be married but — but Giles broke it off almost two years ago while he was in South America."

"He was in the service?" Sam was watching her in that disconcerting, intent way again.

"It was some kind of hush-hush type of thing, I think," Adria said. "I haven't seen him since we broke up."

"I take it you cared a lot for this guy," Sam said, his eyes behind the blank shield of the dark glasses seemed steady on her.

Adria looked away from his gaze and stroked Sarge, who had stretched out near her, enjoying the bits of food passed to him from time to time.

"Yes, I cared a great deal for him," she admitted, "but evidently he didn't feel the same way. It has been difficult getting over him." Suddenly she realized that she was talking much too freely to this stranger and she picked up the aluminum container holding the chicken and held it out to him, "More chicken?"

"No thanks," Sam said. His intent gaze had not left her. "You aren't still waiting for this guy, I hope, not after almost two years."

Adria felt warmth creep up into her cheeks but she lifted her chin slightly and said a little uncertainly, "I-I don't know. So far I haven't gone out much. He was a very special person and maybe I measure everyone by him." Her laugh was forced. "Silly, isn't it, when the guy told me plainly he no longer cared for me."

Sam's next words came slowly, "Some things could happen to a man that would make it impossible for him to marry the one he loves. Maybe that's what happened to your boyfriend."

"Like what?" Adria said. For some inexplicable reason she suddenly felt prickly and argumentative.

She had faced toward him again and saw him still watching her with that watchful, intent way. "A woman who really loves a man would want to share his life regardless of what happened to him!"

"There are some things a man might not want to bring to a marriage, things that might cause his spouse to hate him after a while, or might even be harmful to her. Or maybe she would marry him out of pity, and what man would want that?" Sam said.

"Or maybe my ever-loving fiancé found a new lady love over in that exotic setting," Adria said acidly.

Suddenly Sam unfolded his frame to stand tall and straight. He shrugged. "It happens I'm sure, but frankly I can't see a man giving up a pretty young lady like you — even if she throws spines from her tongue like a porcupine does from his tail."

His levity loosened the tension that held Adria and she giggled, "A porcupine doesn't throw spines, he slaps his tail and drives spines into his unlucky victim."

"Ouch," Sam said. "That's what I thought happened to me when I defended your probably far-from-worthy ex-fiancé."

It was about three-thirty that afternoon when Sam left Adria on the path near the cave. He had his drawings. They had even found another new flower for his collection. As he went up the trail, after thanking her for helping him, she heard him whistling softly. She could have sworn it was "I Dream of Jeannie with the Light Brown Hair."

As she watched him go sadness tugged at her heart. She might never see him again, he had not even asked for her phone number. But she shrugged it off and moved down the path toward The Lodge. Watch it, she warned herself. You don't need to become involved with an unsaved man anyway.

"I've had an enjoyable day and I don't even feel badly about going home to Albuquerque now. Could the fact that Sam lives in Albuquerque have anything to do with you not minding to return there?" she scolded herself aloud. At the same time, she was wondering if she would ever see him there.

For the rest of the day she helped Sarah and Sibyl prepare long Blue-Lake green beans for canning. Just before dark, she went out to the garden and helped Fritz gather fresh corn for their evening meal. They had almost finished stripping the shucks and silks from the ears, dropping the plump, pale-yellow kerneled ears into an enamel kettle when they heard the whine of a car engine on the road.

"Sounds like Kandy and Gentry coming home," Adria said as she reached for the last ear of fresh corn. She started to peel back the moist shuck when Fritz said in his raspy voice, "He's coming too fast."

Adria continued to unwrap the corn but turned toward the sound of the car engine, rapidly getting louder. She now heard the tires screaming on the curves and the spewing of gravel from the tortured tires.

"Something's wrong!" Fritz snapped out, and began to run toward the house. Adria dropped the unfinished ear into the kettle and sprinted after him, her heart beating wildly. Their feet gained the graveled path and both charged around the house and came out into the wide front lawn as Gentry's car spun into the driveway, scattering gravel as it ground to a quick stop.

Gentry jumped from the car, ran around to the passenger side, jerked open the door and bent to lift someone from the car. Adria felt her knees almost buckle. Even in the paling light, Adria had seen the anguish and fear on Gentry's face. Was that dark stain on his shoulder blood?

"Dear God, help!"

Chapter 16

Kandy leaned back in Gentry's luxurious Lincoln Continental and smiled to herself. She dearly loved Adria and had even enjoyed having her accompany Gentry and herself on some of their jaunts this week but today she was glad — very glad — that she had Gentry all to herself.

As if he read her mind, Gentry reached over and covered her slim, tanned hand with his own large strong one. When she turned to look at him, his warm hazel-green eyes crinkled at the corners as he said softly, "That cousin of yours is a fun girl but I'm glad it's just you and me today."

Kandy laughed lightly and snuggled her hand more closely into his. "You know what? I am too."

For a few minutes he drove in silence. Then abruptly he pulled the car far to the side of the road and parked. He turned to Kandy, swallowed hard and said in a rush, "You must know how I feel about you by this time. Perhaps it's too soon to talk about love but I know how I feel and weeks and months will not alter my feelings."

He took a deep, steadying breath, "So I

might as well just say it right out. I love you, Kandy, and I want to marry you if you will have me!"

Kandy felt happiness swell up inside her like a huge, multi-colored balloon. When Gentry spoke the magic words — I love you — the balloon burst inside her and sent out delicious rays, almost maddening waves of joy coursing through her veins and out into every little capillary, until it seemed even the tips of her fingers and toes tingled with happiness.

She didn't answer immediately but ran her eyes lovingly over his radiant, perspiring face. Then very gently she reached over and touched her lips to his. "I love you too, Gentry," she murmured against his warm lips.

All morning they wandered about the streets of Taos, hand in hand, stopping now and then in a sequestered spot to exchange a rapturous kiss. Gentry asked Kandy to come to Coppercrest soon to meet his family.

They were sitting on a bench in a little park-like spot of grass sipping cold drinks and watching the colorful crowds surge by when a sadness came to Gentry's eyes. "I wish you could have met John Howard, the man who raised me and I thought was my father until a while back. But he had a heart attack and died six weeks ago. He was a good man and a good father."

"I'm so sorry."

"You know, it's strange how life is," Gentry said. "Cyrus my natural father has been to the brink of death often in the last several years while Dad seemed to be in robust health. Now Dad is gone and Cyrus is still living, perhaps is even in better health."

"You said Cyrus has recently come to know the Lord. Maybe that accounts for his better health."

"Perhaps it does. His pride and joy is Steven, Lee's little boy and Cyrus' only grandchild. I'm anxious for you to meet my family."

Kandy sighed, "It's scary thinking of meeting your family. I'm just a small town girl and a forest ranger to boot. I know more how to act in the woods than in a mansion."

"You'll like my family," Gentry assured her, "and they'll love you."

"I hope so."

"Elliot Fleet, my stepbrother, and his wife Lee live at Coppercrest so it will be perfectly proper for you to visit. And my mother will be as bad as Sibyl when it comes to fattening you up. You'll love Mom."

As they left the bench and strolled toward Larry's gift shop, Kandy suddenly thought, at least today I haven't been searching every face, looking for my attacker. This is the first time today that his presence in Taos has entered my mind.

Ever since she had seen the blond, bearded young man near her brother's shop several days before, she had caught herself watching for him again. Gentry had noticed it and had assured her of his protection. Gentry's presence made her feel safe, but she still was not able to suppress a shudder whenever she thought of him, even now.

Gentry, walking beside her with her arm tucked in his, felt the slight quiver that ran over her. "You're thinking of that guy again, aren't you?" he said.

She nodded and he said thoughtfully, "You know, I will feel safer when I have you away from Taos for good. I'm still not convinced that the attack on you was a random attack. And I wonder if Larry doesn't know more than he's telling. He seemed awfully mad at that guy."

Kandy shook her head slowly, "I thought so at first but Larry seems relaxed and not worried about a thing anymore so maybe it was as he said — just a petty argument about a petty gambling debt."

"Maybe," Gentry said doubtfully and dropped the subject.

That afternoon they drove west of Taos, on Highway 64, to Angel Fire ski-slopes to ride the ski-lift. Swinging high in the chair-lifts was exhilarating and the scenery was breathtaking.

"This mountain air gives me a prodigious appetite," Gentry said when they were back in the car and headed for home.

"I could use some of Sibyl's good food too," Kandy said. "I believe she said we were having Mexican food tonight."

They had turned off the highway onto the graveled road that wound through the mountains to The Lodge. As he drove slowly along a ridge, Kandy looked far down into a canyon on her side and then said, "I hope Adria wasn't too lonesome today."

"I think she's taking a lot of interest in that guy who's camped out on your land, you know the one she told us about that's doing a book for nature lovers?"

"Oh yes, Sam I believe she called him. I surely hope Adria does get interested in someone else. Giles has been out of her life for close to two years and she just can't seem to give him up in her heart."

"That Giles must have been quite a man for her to cling to his memory like that."

"He really was," Kandy said earnestly. "He and Adria seemed so perfect for each other and he seemed absolutely crazy about her. I can't imagine why he broke off with her."

"Probably met someone else," Gentry said, "It happens. . . ." A sharp crack sounded very near and a hole appeared in the windshield on Kandy's side, spattering both of them with bits of safety glass. Gentry, braking the car hard, heard Kandy gasp and turning his head saw her hands convulsively clutching at her left shoulder, a red stain spilling out between her brown fingers.

Gentry brought the car to a frenzied halt, pulled on the hand brake and was leaning toward Kandy when he heard another sharp report and felt the whistle of a bullet past his head. Before his horrified eyes, he saw Kandy flinch and then with a soft moan, she fell forward in the seat.

Gentry's terror for Kandy galvanized him into action. He pushed Kandy gently to the floor and lay down in the seat above her. Someone was out there who seemed deadly intent on murdering Kandy. Someone who would likely be at the car door any minute to finish his job. If he hadn't already succeeded! Then, with vast relief, Gentry heard

Kandy's labored breathing and heard her moan softly.

Gentry raised up and peered over the dash. His own breath came loud to his ears as he strained to see into the thick growth of trees and brush which crowded the road on both sides. The ambush had been planned perfectly. The shooter had been lying in wait where Gentry had slowed the car as it swung around the sharp bend into a tunnel of deep underbrush and trees.

The sound of Kandy's continued breathing was music to his ears as he crouched over her and watched and listened. At least Kandy was alive. Nothing stirred out there now.

Hoping that the ambusher had fled, he gently turned Kandy so he could see her face. Her body was limp and unresponsive, her bloody hands no longer clutched at her left shoulder. On her left temple a long bloody groove creased her head.

Then his heart almost stopped. Bright crimson was pumping steadily from a neat hole in her blouse near her shoulder. Moving as if in a fog of anguished shock, Gentry quickly transferred a plump pillow from the back seat to the front and rested Kandy's head against it. Rapidly he rolled his windbreaker into a ball and pushed it against the pulsing, scarlet flow in her shoulder.

His whole body seemed to be vibrating, hot blood pounding in his head, icy fear pulsing through his veins. He had to get help for Kandy, but if he took away the pressure on her wound, Kandy's blood would drain from her body and she would die. An anguished sob broke from his twisted lips. "Dear Father, don't let Kandy die. I-I love her more than life itself!

"I-I've got to think rationally," his muttered words seemed to partly still the panic breaking over him in waves of tidal wave proportion.

Keeping the pressure firm on the wound, Gentry eased his right hand over the wound and removed his left. Sweeping the sides of the road with a quick flick of his head, he saw no movement. He eased over into the driver's seat as far as he could and still keep pressure on Kandy's wound. Thank God, the engine was still going.

"Father God, protect Kandy from further harm from the gunman," he prayed fervently as he eased the car into motion.

No further gunfire bursts met them although Gentry expected one any minute all the way to The Lodge. He had to drive hunched over and tensed to keep pressure on Kandy's shoulder. Most of the time, he talked to her — wildly at times, he recalled later — begging her to not die, urging her to hold on to life, telling her how much he loved her.

His body was aching with fatigue and tension by the time he swung into The Lodge drive. He ran the car as close to the gate of the yard fence as possible. Releasing the pressure on Kandy's wound, he leaped from the car and ran to the other side.

Grabbing a car robe from the back he flipped it out onto the ground and leaned in to lift Kandy from the car.

Dimly he was aware that others were around him as he lowered her to the blanket and thrust the bloody wadded-up windbreaker against the wound again. "Call 911! Get help for Kandy," he heard himself shouting. "She's been shot!"

Gentry's breath was coming in gasps, his face was ashen. Larry's voice spoke at his side, "Let me relieve you." Then Larry was pressing the ball of windbreaker against the wound.

He heard Adria's voice, "Sibyl is calling 911. What happened?" Her voice broke, but after a quick undrawn breath, she asked, "Who did this? What happened?"

Before Gentry could get his wits together

enough to answer, firm hands were gently pushing Gentry aside and Fritz's raspy voice spoke in his ear, "Move over there a mite and let me see."

Gentry moved aside and saw that Fritz was taking bandages from a small red and white first-aid kit. Ripping a package open, Fritz had Larry lift the make-shift pressure-bandage and he flipped a heavy sterile bandage onto the wound and covered it with a heavy folded piece of clean white sheet.

"Put pressure on that again." Only a slight tremor in his voice betrayed Fritz's anxiety.

Larry complied, his face set and white.

Fritz moved to the long cut on the side of Kandy's head. With relief, Gentry saw it wasn't bleeding nearly as badly as the wound in her shoulder. The handyman applied a wide sterile bandage over it and wound a long bandage about her head to hold it in place.

Sibyl came swiftly across the lawn, her short stout legs churning. Opening the gate she panted over to them. "The paramedics will be here soon." She carried a blanket which Fritz spread over Kandy's lower body.

Sarah arrived then with a basin of water and Fritz gently sponged away the blood from Kandy's face and hands.

Adria tugged at Gentry's arm and asked in a tight, unnatural voice, "Who did this? What happened?"

"I-I don't know," Gentry said. "We were going around a curve in the road and suddenly I heard the sound of a shot and a hole was in the windshield, glass was everywhere and-and blood was running from Kandy's shoulder. I slammed on the brakes and then as I leaned to help Kandy another bullet struck her.

"Her-her head fell to the side when we stopped so sudden . . ." Gentry choked, swallowed hard, then continued in a constricted voice, "If she hadn't moved her head, the shot would have hit her right in the center of her forehead."

Larry, who had now been relieved by Fritz, stood to his feet. Staring at Gentry with horror-filled eyes, he spoke so low it was hard to distinguish the words, "The man was a crack shot, wasn't he?"

"I would say he was aiming only at Kandy and hit what he aimed at," Gentry said in a harsh, quivering voice.

"The bearded, blond man that Kandy thought beat her up! The one Kandy saw in town the other day. It must have been him who shot her!" Adria exclaimed. Her eyes

174

were wide and staring as she hovered near Kandy's figure lying so still upon the ground.

Suddenly to their ears came the faint sound of a siren and Sibyl said unnecessarily, "The rescue unit is coming." Within minutes, Kandy was in the capable hands of the paramedics and it wasn't long until the ambulance screamed away, with Adria, Larry, Sibyl and Gentry following in Gentry's car.

The night was a long one. Kandy was taken immediately into surgery and the hours lengthened out impossibly long and nerve racking. Finally a surgeon appeared and told them the bullet was out and Kandy's condition, though extremely critical, had improved.

"She has a chance," he said. "Certainly a better one than I first had feared. But she is far from out of danger," he cautioned. "She seems in excellent health, though, and that is a definite plus.

"I would advise you all to get some rest because Miss Graham is being well cared for and there is nothing more you can do here."

Gentry, however, refused to go. His voice was piteous as he confided to the family, "I asked Kandy to be my wife just today, and she accepted." His face twisted with anguish and his shoulders began to shake. Larry laid a hand on his shoulder in silent sympathy and Adria said softly, "She's going to make it, Gentry. She's got to. We all love her too much to let her go."

"And we don't plan to leave Kandy either, Gentry," Sibyl said stoutly.

After a minute, Gentry straightened his shoulders and wiped his face. "If they have a chapel, I want to talk to God about this."

"I'll show you where," Adria said gently and they moved down the hall.

When they had gone, Sibyl took Larry by the arm and led him to a sofa. "I want to talk to you," she said. "What did Adria mean when she said Kandy thought she had seen the man who attacked her? Why didn't anyone tell me that!"

Larry stiffened and he said quickly, "Oh, Kandy saw a blond bearded man over in Taos that she seemed convinced was the one who beat her."

"But you don't think he was the one? Do you know this man?"

Larry did not quite meet her eyes, "He's someone I met somewhere, don't know him very well, though. And no, I don't think he beat Kandy up."

"But Kandy was sure he was the one who attacked her?"

"Yes, but the man who assaulted her was smooth-shaven and this man has a heavy beard."

"Any man could grow a beard," Sibyl said.

"But don't you see," Larry said earnestly, "how could Kandy know he was her attacker when she could hardly even see his face? That's why I can't believe he was the man."

"Tell me exactly what she said about him," Sibyl persisted.

Irritation glimmered in Larry's dark eyes, "She said the man's eyes were terrifying or something like that, just like the man's who hurt her. Does that seem logical to you — that she could recognize her assailant by how his eyes looked?"

For a long moment Sibyl stared at Larry, "What's this bearded man's name?"

"Oh, I don't know, Sibyl," Larry said indifferently. "What does it matter?"

"What does it matter? What does it matter!" Sibyl's voice had risen and now she glared at him. "Because the man may have tried to murder your sister, that's why!"

Larry's eyes narrowed and he spoke stiffly, "What will we tell the police? That we think a man with wild, terrifying eyes tried to kill our sister, when Gentry said he didn't even get a glimpse of the one who shot her?"

"Why are you afraid to tell me the name of this friend of yours that Kandy thought might have attacked her?"

"He isn't my friend, just someone I met," Larry said angrily. "I just don't think we should start making accusations, that's all. It could get us into deep trouble."

"One of us is already in trouble — she might even die," Sibyl said severely. "Now tell me the name of that man!"

"Otto," Larry said grudgingly.

"Otto Colman?" Sibyl asked.

"Sure, Otto Colman; how did you know his last name."

"Our father tried to send him to prison for burglary two or three years ago," Sibyl said, "but he was released on a technicality."

Larry's eyes widened, "I didn't know that!"

"I kept up with many of Father's cases," she said. "Remember, he always depended on me, even discussed his cases with me sometimes."

"You think Otto might be trying to get even with Dad for trying to put him away?"

"Perhaps," Sibyl said thoughtfully. "I plan to try to find out."

Chapter 17

After spending the night at the hospital, the family left early the next morning to go back to The Lodge to clean up and change clothes. Kandy had not regained consciousness but seemed to be resting.

Larry returned to Taos as soon as he had bathed and had a quick breakfast. He needed to open the shop and get extra help, and planned to return to the hospital as soon as possible. Gentry also tarried only long enough to take a shower, shave and change, not even stopping to eat breakfast.

Adria called the hospital and when informed there was no change in Kandy's condition, managed to persuade Sibyl to rest for a couple of hours before going back to the hospital. After a quick bath, Adria lay down, thinking she could at least rest her eyes. She prayed for a few minutes and was surprised to wake almost three hours later when Sibyl called her.

"I've called the hospital and Kandy is still the same," Sibyl said, "but I would like to go down now. Maybe if they let us talk to her, it will help rouse her."

Sibyl insisted on taking her old station

wagon instead of driving down with Adria. "I have some errands to do," she explained.

When they arrived at the hospital, Gentry was sitting in a small waiting room not far from Kandy's room. He looked terrible, with bloodshot eyes and haggard face. He said Kandy was still unconscious. Adria asked if he had slept any and he confessed he hadn't.

"You need to rest some," Sibyl said gently. "Kandy needs you well, not sick."

"I know," Gentry said, "but that awful scene keeps rolling over and over in my mind like a film. I've lived every moment of the shooting a hundred times."

"I'm sorry," Adria said, laying her hand on his arm and squeezing gently. "But you need to put it in God's hands, if you can."

"I-I keep thinking that some way I should have protected her. She was afraid of that guy and I assured her she was safe because I would protect her," Gentry said bitterly.

"You think that bearded man Kandy saw in Taos shot her then?" Sibyl asked sharply.

"Who else could it have been?" Gentry said. "She's had the jitters ever since she saw him the other day."

"Larry said he doesn't think Kandy could have possibly identified that man as her attacker because his face was covered with a beard," Sibyl said.

"And I think Larry is hiding something," Gentry said explosively. Anger glinted in his eyes. "When Kandy saw that guy he was having a bang-up argument with Larry. And when we went into his office directly afterward, Larry looked like his world had caved in around him."

"Larry never told me about any of that," Sibyl said slowly.

Gentry was obviously trying to bring his temper under control but he spoke through tightly compressed lips, "Kandy asked Larry what was the matter with him and Larry gave a lame story about his stomach being upset. Nobody ever looked that wiped-out from a stomach ache."

"Was that when Kandy said she thought the man had been her assailant?" Sibyl asked.

"Yes, and Larry took up for him and hooted at Kandy's assertion when she said she knew the man was her attacker because his eyes had blazed with kind of a wild light when he looked at her in passing, like the man's did who beat her so badly."

"Did she think the man recognized her?" Sibyl pressed.

"She was positive he did," Gentry said. "That's why she has been afraid, looking into the face of every blond man we passed all this week, searching for the man. Until yesterday! We were both so happy, we almost completely forgot about him." His voice shook and he muttered something about needing to get some air and hurried away.

"Poor man," Sibyl said, watching his tall, powerful figure until he disappeared down the stairs, "He's so in love with our Kandy. It just doesn't seem fair, they have just found each other."

When they passed the nurses' station, a trim young nurse hurried out to intercept them, "I've been watching for you. The police chief has called for you twice. You are to call this number." Thrusting a card into Sibyl's hand, she hurried back to her desk.

"You call and talk to them," Sibyl said. "I hate that sort of thing. I thought they talked to us all enough last night. I'll go on in and sit with Kandy." She gave Adria the card and hurried around the corner.

Adria quickly located a public phone and placed the call. It must be important, she thought, when the officer who answered said the chief wanted to talk to her personally and said he would buzz him. Almost immediately the chief came on the phone.

"We have good news, Miss Graham," he

said as soon as Adria identified herself, "We have the one who shot your cousin. His name is Sam Tillet."

"Sam Tillet? Are you sure?" Adria asked in utter astonishment.

"Yes," the chief said triumphantly. "We found the gun, a .270 Winchester, wrapped in an old blanket hidden in his vehicle. Two shots were fired from it and the bullet taken from your cousin's body came from that gun."

"Are-are Sam's fingerprints on the gun?"

"No, it's been wiped clean but that's to be expected. I'm sure he planned to get rid of the gun but we caught him before he could."

"Does Sam admit to the crime," Adria asked dazedly.

"No, of course not, but he was just pulling out when we got there and he really made a fight of it when we tried to take him in." He chuckled grimly, "In fact, he tossed us around like match sticks until I laid him out with a night stick."

As the police chief spoke the part about Sam tossing the officers around like match sticks, Adria saw vividly in her mind the picture of her admirer in Albuquerque as he scattered the men who had been badgering her. He had tossed those men around like they were rag dolls. And the man had been tall and reed thin, too, just as Sam was! Was Sam her mysterious champion?

She could hear the chief's voice asking her a question.

"Miss — Miss, are you still there?" When she assured him that she was, he went on, "It sounds like you know Sam Tillet. Is he a friend of the family?"

"No — no, he is just a man who has been camping out in our woods, doing some drawings of wildflowers for a book. I might have seen him around Albuquerque too, but I'm not sure."

Adria was struggling to deal with this. "Are you positive Sam Tillet shot my cousin," she said faintly. "I met him out in the woods and he seemed like such a nice guy."

"A lot of murderers are," the officer said dryly. "But this guy seems to have mental problems."

"Mental problems?"

"Yes, we had him checked out and it seems he was hurt while he was a prisoner of war, he was a soldier, and he sometimes goes berserk. Once in the hospital he broke the jaw of an orderly when he had one of those spells."

Adria felt her knees go weak. "But-but what motive could he have had for shooting my cousin?"

"A guy like that wouldn't need one. He's imbalanced anyway."

When Adria hung up she couldn't remember if she had thanked the chief for keeping them informed or not. Her head was spinning and she felt nauseous and sick. She found a bathroom and sat down in a chair for a few minutes while her stomach and head slowly returned to normal.

Sam Tillet — a murderer? Could it be possible? She had spent time with him and although he seemed a little odd, he had seemed so intelligent and likable. But if he just went berserk now and then, he might appear quite normal the rest of the time.

For some inexplicable reason, Adria felt like crying, in fact, she felt like bawling her eyes out! For suddenly she realized that Sam had stirred feeling in her that only Giles had been able to rouse. This was the man she had hoped to get to know better!

And the man had attempted to kill her cousin! He was a mental case! "Oh, you know how to pick them, don't you," she told herself scornfully. "First Giles who dumped you, probably for some pretty Spanish girl, and then you pick a kook who goes on the rampage every once in a while and tosses people around and shot my dear cousin to-to pieces!"

She was sobbing now and suddenly she felt a hand on her shoulder and looked up shamefacedly into the sympathetic face of a nurse. "Are you all right, Miss?"

Adria stammered out that she was and hastily dried her tears on a tissue that the nurse supplied from her uniform pocket.

"You're related to that girl who was brought in shot last night, aren't you?" the nurse said.

When Adria nodded her head, the nurse said smilingly, "You might want to go up and see her. She just regained consciousness a few minutes ago."

Adria jumped up, hugged the startled nurse and dashed out the door and down the hall. After a few running steps she slowed down, however. People were staring at her and besides she had almost run down a big white-garbed orderly.

Chapter 18

When Adria came near the door of Kandy's room, a stern faced, iron-gray haired nurse came out. When Adria told her she was part of the family, the nurse gave her permission to go in for a couple of minutes. "She will need to rest," she said protectively. "And please do not talk to her about the shooting. When she is stronger there will be plenty of time to talk about that."

Adria tiptoed in. Kandy lay so still and white that for a moment Adria felt like fleeing. Sibyl stood at her side with Kandy's hand in hers. A tremulous smile quivered on her lips. "She's awake and knew me," she whispered. "Thank God!"

Kandy's dark eyes fluttered open and her colorless lips curved into a weak smile, "Hi, Adria." Her eyes closed wearily for a moment, then opened again and her lips trembled. "What happened to me? No one will tell me anything! Where is Gentry?" A wild look came in her eyes, "Is Gentry okay? Please tell me!"

"I'm right here, honey," Gentry said from the doorway. His face still looked worn and exhausted but his face shone like the noonday sun. In two steps he was across the room. Adria stepped back and he leaned over the bed and touched his lips lightly to Kandy's.

Her hand lifted tremulously to touch his face. "I dreamed something had happened to you," she whispered weakly. Her expression was puzzled. "That you were shot or something." Then her countenance smoothed to one of peace, "It doesn't matter. Now that I know you're all right, I can rest." Her eyelids closed, tried to reopen and then with a little contented sigh, she slept.

The nurse was beckoning them from the doorway and they slipped out. "Sleep is what she needs most right now," the nurse said.

"But can't I sit with her," Gentry cajoled, "If I promise to not wake her up?"

The nurse studied Gentry, then her gimlet eyes softened. "If you will promise me you will try to sleep a little. There's a comfortable chair in there. You look awful!"

She turned to the others, "You may peek in now and then but no talking!" With back ramrod stiff, she moved away down the hall.

"Thank God, Kandy's awake," Gentry whispered. "I was afraid the shot to her head might have put her in a coma."

He reached out to squeeze Sibyl and Adria's hands and then went back into the room.

A few minutes later Adria and Sibyl were in a small waiting room near Kandy's room, when a pudgy, balding little man approached them. "Are you Adria and Sibyl Graham?" he asked.

"Yes," Adria answered, "I'm Adria and this is my cousin, Sibyl."

The kindly gentleman shook hands with them and introduced himself as Mason Keeley. "I'm the lawyer representing Sam Tillet," he explained. "I would like to ask you some questions, Miss Adria Graham, if you don't mind."

"Did Sam Tillet shoot my sister?" Sibyl asked quickly.

Mr. Keeley's answer was kind but firm, "No, Miss Graham, I do not believe for a minute that he did."

"But the police said he was found with the weapon, and resisted arrest when they tried to bring him in for questioning," Adria said.

"Purely circumstantial evidence. My client's fingerprints were not found on the gun," the little man explained, "and —" he hesitated, "my client has a little problem when surrounded with men with guns. He was hurt in combat and was a prisoner for a period of time, so when the officers surrounded him he thought the enemy was trying to capture him and he panicked."

"Maybe he thought Kandy was the enemy also, so he shot her," Sibyl said.

"No way!" the attorney said emphatically. "Sam is perfectly lucid unless a sudden situation such as this occurs. He would never stalk someone or set up an ambush to kill a woman in a car."

"How do you know that?" Adria said. "If he can go berserk in an instant why could he not ambush someone, thinking they were the enemy."

But Mason was shaking his head, "No, the attacks only last for a few seconds or a few minutes at most, then his mind takes control again and he is as sane as anyone. It would have taken time to plan and carry out an ambush like the one Gentry Howard described to the police last night. The gunman was lying in wait for them at a strategic spot, and I might add, the shooter obviously was aiming at the girl. My client fought with men in combat so why would he fire at a woman?"

"You tell us!" Sibyl said belligerently.

"My client is a law-abiding man whose only desire at this point is to finish the book he is working on," the lawyer said patiently. "He did not shoot Kandy Graham. In fact, he spoke very highly of you Grahams for not running him off your property when you knew he was camped there. Why would he want to repay your kindness by trying to kill one of you."

"Someone tried to kill my sister!" Sibyl said.

"Yes, of course someone did and that's what we are trying to find out: who did the shooting." He turned to Adria, "Mr. Tillet would like to talk to you."

"Why does he want to talk to me?" asked Adria. She shrank from facing the man who very possibly shot Kandy, with murder in mind. And one who might go berserk at any minute and try to kill me too, she thought with a shudder. She also admitted to herself that she was reluctant to face the man she had felt drawn to and was so wrong about. What could he want of her now?

"He didn't say, but perhaps we can come up with some answers if you talk face to face with him. Would you come down to the jail and talk with him? Please," his attorney urged.

Adria agreed even though Sibyl expressed her disapproval.

Adria declined Mr. Keeley's offer to drive

her but followed him in her own car. Sibyl stayed at the hospital so she would be near Kandy.

A short while later Adria was ushered into a small room where she faced Sam down the length of a table, out of his reach, she realized gratefully. The lawyer sat at the side of the table. She was horrified to see that Sam's feet and hands were shackled with chains, then she experienced relief. The police were making certain the man could not attack anyone.

Sam's face was pale and he needed a shave but his eyes were still covered with those irritating dark glasses. The old slouch hat was still clamped down over his curling dark hair. A large, dark bruise disfigured one cheekbone, running up under the sun glasses. She recalled the policeman had said Sam had been subdued with a night stick and strangely she felt sympathy for the shackled prisoner.

For a moment Adria and Sam just stared at each other and then Sam made a deprecating motion with his hand and the chains clinked. Adria winced.

"This is a fine kettle of fish, isn't it," Sam said with a crooked, definitely embarrassed grin. "I haven't been in chains since I was a prisoner of war."

"Did you shoot Kandy?" Adria asked abruptly.

"Of course I didn't shoot your cousin!" Sam said explosively. "What possible motive would I have had?"

When Adria was silent but continued to stare — a little defiantly — into the blankness of the dark glasses, he dropped his head to study his chained hands for a moment.

"Please believe me," he said, lifting his head, "I did not shoot Kandy, didn't even hear the shots. I had packed up and carried everything over to the road where my Bronco was parked. When everything was stowed away, I started off and then the cops showed up and stopped me."

"The police said the gun that shot Kandy was found in your vehicle," Adria said.

"Sure! And how it got there I have no idea — but it would have been easy for anyone to have put that gun in my vehicle to make me appear guilty! I was camped over a little rise from my truck."

"You saw no one near your Bronco?"

"Not a soul, but I didn't go near the vehicle after I left you until the next morning. And the police said the shooting was later on in the evening after you and I got back from looking for the flowers you told me about."

"But wouldn't you have noticed something as big as a rifle in your vehicle?"

"I was more surprised than the cops when they found a gun in my truck," Sam said. "It was found between the seats, wrapped in an old blanket and covered with an old tarp, both mine that I always carry in my Bronco."

"Sam's fingerprints aren't on the gun," Mason Keeley interposed. "It had been wiped clean."

"Of course you might have wiped it clean and planned to dispose of the weapon as soon as you got out of our area," Adria said.

Sam swiped his chained hand across his forehead in apparent exasperation and the chains clinked together like a death toll. His battered old hat tilted on his head, then fell off onto the floor. Before the attorney rescued it and set it back on its owner's head, Adria saw Sam's head and froze.

The thick, dark brown, sweat-dampened wavy mane, the well formed head and close fitting ears, and the strong white forehead were so much like Giles's that she caught her breath in dismay. If only she could see his eyes! Giles's eyes were dark-lashed and pale gray that could lighten and darken according to his moods.

Of course this was not Giles. This man's

chin was rounded, his nose was straight, and his cheekbones were not pronounced. Giles's chin had been square, his cheekbones high like an Indian's and his nose had a hump. Sam also had deep lines etched near eyes and mouth and just a touch of gray at the temples and Giles did not.

"Are you memorizing what a would-be murderer looks like?" Sam said with a cynical laugh.

Adria felt her face blaze and dropped her eyes. "Sorry, I didn't realize I was staring. You just remind me of-of a man I used to know."

Sam's chuckle was not mirthful, "Not your faithless Giles Hughlet, I hope?"

Adria's head came up and she said coldly, "I do not know that Giles was unfaithful to me and besides, I don't wish to discuss Giles!" Skewering him with storm-gray eyes, she said testily, "It's you we were discussing."

Sam drew in a deep breath, "Sorry, I didn't mean to offend you." He glanced at his attorney, "Would you mind to tell Mr. Keeley how you came to my camp and why?"

Adria related how she had found the cache of guns and the camping equipment in the cave and how she had presumed they belonged to the man she had heard whistling earlier.

"So when you visited Sam's camp you didn't find any weapons, except the old .22 pistol in Sam's food box?" Keeley asked.

"That is correct," Adria said. "And the camping gear was not the things I found in the cave. Mr. Tillet's are much used and his tent was green and the other one was bright blue."

"Would you be willing to tell that to the police?" Keeley asked.

"Certainly," Adria said. "However, I'm sure you realize that Sam could have had two outfits of camping gear."

"Only I don't," Sam said emphatically. "Have the police check it out. Why would I have two sets of camping stuff?"

"I'm not saying you did," Adria said defensively. Suddenly she had a new thought. "What about that man you said you saw in the woods? Remember? Did you mention that to the police?"

"I certainly did but they didn't seem to give it any credence. I suppose they think I will say anything to get the heat off of me."

"What did he look like?" Adria asked.

Sam considered, "I didn't get too good a look at him. He was walking fast away from me, over on the slope not too far from your cave. And he didn't even pause when I called good morning to him."

"Describe him as best you can," Adria said.

"He was tall, athletic-looking, with light-colored hair, no hat. I believe I glimpsed a blondish beard."

"Was he carrying anything?"

"No, but I do recall that he wore a tan jacket and dark pants. When I came close to where he had walked, I noticed his footprint — a hiking boot, I think — had a distinctive leaf pattern."

Adria sat silent and thoughtful for a moment and then said slowly, "A few days ago Kandy thought she saw the man who beat her up a couple of years ago."

"In Taos?" Sam asked.

"Yes, and she thought he recognized her. She described him as tall, well-built, blond and has a beard, like the man you saw in the forest."

"You mean you think the man might be afraid she would make trouble for him and he tried to kill her?" Keeley asked.

"I don't want to speculate but Gentry's wondering if there wasn't more to Kandy being attacked than a random, unplanned beating, but he doesn't have too much to go on for his conjecture."

"Have you told the police about Kandy thinking she recognized her attacker in Taos?" Keeley asked.

"Yes, we told them but I'm afraid they were pretty skeptical because he looked so different. You see, the man who attacked her was smooth-shaven, with close-cropped hair, and this man wears a full covering beard and longish hair."

"How did she recognize the man?" Sam asked.

"Kandy said his eyes were the same and when he saw her they seemed to flame up with a wild light — just like the man's did when he was beating her."

"Even if Miss Graham is right, I'm afraid a jury would be skeptical of just recognizing a man by how his eyes looked when he saw her," Keeley said slowly.

Adria stood to her feet. "I know. Well, I had better go and I will tell the police that I didn't see that Winchester in your camp when I visited it. That's all I can do for you."

The attorney stood and extended his hand, "Thank you for seeing my client."

Sam also stood, with a clinking of chains. His voice held a pleading intensity, "You do believe that I didn't harm your cousin, don't you?"

Adria stared into the dark glasses briefly, then said slowly, "I'm not sure if I can believe you. You haven't been completely honest with me."

"In what way," Sam's lawyer was quick to ask.

Adria still looked into Sam's face, "I believe you knew me before I met you in the woods. Aren't you the man who rescued me from those hoodlums that night about a month ago?"

Sam's body seemed to go rigid — and still. When he didn't answer, Adria went on in a sharper voice, "And you have followed me around Albuquerque ever since, even standing across the street every night to watch my apartment window until I turn out my light."

"Is that true?" Keeley asked in a voice edged with anger.

When Sam continued to stand stiffly silent, his attorney said impatiently, "As your lawyer, it is imperative that you come completely clean with me about everything! Is Miss Graham's accusation true? Had you met Miss Graham back in Albuquerque? Did you follow her around, spying on her?" His words were like sharp projectiles shot out into the deep silence.

Sam shifted his weight, with a clinking of

his shackles, and sighed. "Yes, I did know Adria — Miss Graham. But I never spied upon her."

"What would you call it, then?" Adria asked bitingly. "I greatly appreciated you rescuing me from those men but that gave you no right to follow me about like-like some kind of weirdo!"

Sam's voice was grave as he said softly, "I'm sorry if I scared you. I would never harm you — not ever! You must believe that."

"What is your reason for following this young lady about, even to her apartment every night?" Keeley asked caustically.

Sam's voice sounded weary, "My reason has nothing to do with what I'm charged with — shooting Miss Graham's cousin."

"A judge and jury will make much of your following the shooting victim's cousin around in Albuquerque!" Keeley said sarcastically. "If you knew this young lady perhaps you knew the other one too, and they both had some kind of weird fascination for you."

"That's absolutely ridiculous!" Sam said.

"Just tell me why you followed me everywhere," Adria said as calmly as she could manage. "And where did you meet me? I can't recall ever seeing you before that time you protected me from the ruffians."

"You will just have to accept that I meant you no harm," Sam said in a tight, bitter voice. "I have nothing further to say on the subject."

"How can I defend you when you are withholding information from me," Keeley asked in exasperation.

After a couple of minutes, in which Sam stood stubbornly silent, Adria bade them both a stiff goodbye. Keeley again thanked Adria for coming and Sam unsmilingly echoed his thanks, without looking at her.

As she hurried down the hall behind the guard, Adria pondered. Who was Sam Tillet? Why would he not tell her why he had trailed her about, and another thought kept buzzing around in her brain like a pesky mosquito: Why did Sam Tillet remind her so much of Giles?

His head and hair were exactly like Giles' and his voice, except for a certain huskiness, was much like his. He even did bird-calls and whistled like Giles, even to whistling "I Dream of Jeannie." Again she wished she could see his eyes. Were they also like Giles's?

When she was out on the street once more and headed for her car, her mind resumed her questioning thoughts about Sam. Of course Sam couldn't actually be Giles. The features of his face were different, but was he perhaps related to Giles? Did that account for the attraction the strange man held for her? For attracted she was, she admitted to herself, in spite of the fact that he was a suspect in Kandy's shooting. Every time she was around this guy, her heart did crazy unbidden things.

How ridiculous! she scolded herself. No doubt the man was a kook. He had admitted to being the one who followed her about Albuquerque, for some warped reason of his own. Maybe he had come up here to resume his eerie spying on her and saw Kandy and was attracted to her too, and saw her with someone else and tried to kill her in jealousy!

She put the key in the lock of her car and turned it, then stood for a moment thinking of Sam's soft spoken words: "I'm sorry if I scared you. I would never harm you — not ever! You must believe that."

Adria climbed thoughtfully into her car and started the engine.

The memory of Sam's soft, earnest words set her heart to thumping. For suddenly she realized that she believed Sam. She did not believe he would harm her, even if for some strange reason he had shadowed her in the city.

Could he have shot Kandy? Slowly her head began to shake. No, she did not believe Sam would harm her cousin either. She had nothing concrete to base her feeling on except Sam's denial but it had carried weight — in her heart.

As she drove toward the hospital a sudden thought convulsed her stomach and made her palms slick upon the wheel. If Sam Tillet was not Kandy's would-be assassin, the killer was still out there! He had not succeeded so he would likely try again!

Other thoughts pushed into her mind. Why was this person after Kandy? Was this shooting connected to the attack on Kandy two years before? As far as Adria knew, fun-loving, good natured Kandy didn't have an enemy in the world. Why was she under attack now, and who was her attacker?

Chapter 19

When Adria reached the hospital, she found that Kandy was still sleeping. "Her shoulder pains her some," Gentry said, "but they have given her medication to kill the pain." They walked down to the waiting room together.

"Where is Sibyl," Adria asked, surprised that she was not hovering around Kandy's room.

"Sibyl has gone home," Gentry said. His forehead wrinkled into a slight frown, "She seemed perturbed."

"Do you mean she's worried about Kandy?" Adria asked.

"No, she seemed pleased that Kandy is sleeping peacefully and of the doctor's optimism about her condition. But she made a call to someone and when she came back she looked disturbed."

"That's when she decided to go home?"

"Right. She told me that since Kandy was sleeping anyway that she would go home and come back later in the evening."

"Hmmmm, that's rather unusual for Sibyl," Adria said thoughtfully. "When one of her brood even has a cold, she hovers over them like a little mother hen."

"You don't suppose she resents me staying so close to her little sister, do you?" Gentry said worriedly. "I wouldn't want her to feel I'm pushing in ahead of family."

Adria laughed softly and said emphatically, "I'm sure that's not the problem. Sibyl is delighted about you two!"

She looked at Gentry's tired face and said solicitously, "You look as if you could use some rest. Why don't you go out to The Lodge and get some sleep. Kandy is likely to sleep all day, according to the nurse I talked to on the way in. I'll stay here with Kandy and call you if there is any significant change."

"I've napped a little on a couch in the waiting room," Gentry said, "so I'm doing okay." He grinned somewhat sheepishly, "Maybe I'm like a love-struck teenager but I would really rather stay close to Kandy right now."

He hesitated, "Back to Sibyl, I had the feeling that something was deeply troubling her, after that call. We were sitting out in the waiting room talking and she seemed fine. Then suddenly out of the blue, she said she needed to make a call. And when she returned she looked really troubled — even angry, I'd say."

"She didn't say who she called?"

"No, but she left immediately after

making the call."

"Maybe I should go out and see if something's wrong," Adria said thoughtfully. "Kandy doesn't need me right now." She rose, "You'll call us if there's any change?"

Gentry assured her he would.

When Adria arrived at The Lodge, Sarah told her that Sibyl had gone for a walk. "Up toward that cave, I think."

Adria decided to leave Sarge in the yard this time — in spite of his pathetic whining. If Sibyl was worried about something, Adria didn't want to add to it by bringing Sarge who seemed bent on winning Sibyl by the only way he knew — licking and rubbing against her. "Getting hairs all over me!" Sibyl always complained.

All was quiet and peaceful as Adria neared the cave after the steep climb. Peace, like a balm, laid its healing hand upon Adria as she climbed. Forests always did this to her. "Maybe I should have been a forest ranger too," she mumbled to herself. "The frantic pace and city noises of Albuquerque are not conducive to a peaceful heart."

She paused to rest for a moment under a huge towering pine. But I love the excitement of going after a story, she thought. I would miss that. She started to move on when she heard voices just beyond the bend of the trail ahead. "That's strange," she muttered. Her rubber-soled athletic shoes made no noise as she took the few steps to the bend and peered around.

What she saw didn't register for a few seconds on her brain. When it did, her heart gave a convulsive leap and she slipped to the side of the trail and into the screening brush. Working her way silently forward until she could see without being seen, she studied the two figures who stood above her but just below the entrance to the cave.

A tall muscular-appearing young man stood talking with Sibyl. The stranger's long hair and full beard were blond, very light, and he and Sibyl seemed to be arguing, although they were keeping their voices too low for Adria to hear more than a word now and then. What was going on?

Could this be the man Kandy and Gentry had seen with Larry that day, the man who Kandy was convinced was her attacker? She moved slightly and a prickly branch of a bush nudged Adria's ribs and she jumped and then looked fearfully to see if the two had heard the faint noise she had made.

But the two seemed too absorbed in their debate to notice. The man's voice was low and soothing, Adria more felt than heard, and Sibyl seemed to be the one who was angry. The word "Larry" came to her ears two or three times and Kandy's name at least once.

Suddenly Sibyl turned and began to climb up to the cave entrance. Adria saw that she had changed to her old loose gardening slacks and a checkered, long-sleeved shirt. The man followed Sibyl, carrying a large, flat package like a picture frame. Sibyl pushed aside the screening shrubbery and climbed through. The stranger scrambled after her, and then they were hidden from view. For a moment there was the faint sound of feet scrabbling for holds as they climbed upon the ledge and then there was silence. They were in the cave.

It was an enormous surprise to Adria that Sibyl even knew where the cave was. As far as she knew the woman never climbed or even took walks. For exercise, she worked in her flower beds around The Lodge, raising the gorgeous blooms that appeared in the house in colorful bouquets.

As the moments grew long and the figures didn't reappear, Adria considered climbing up to the cave. Sibyl would have to give her an explanation then, wouldn't she? Did Sibyl know this man's description fitted the one of the fellow Kandy had said Larry was arguing with outside of his gift shop? Kandy and Gentry had said Larry looked positively devastated afterwards in his office.

Maybe there was a logical explanation for Sibyl's tryst with this guy. But if he was the same person, both she and Larry had been arguing with him. Was this the person to whom Sibyl had placed a call in town and had come home immediately to meet here in the woods? It seemed likely. A shudder of fear ran down Adria's spine. Was that man harming Sibyl? They had been in the cave for a very long time.

She glanced at her watch and saw that in reality, they had only been there for ten minutes or so. Adria was considering going back to the house to call for help when she heard sounds from the hidden cave entrance and in a moment the shoulders of the man appeared. He half slid, half climbed down the short stretch of trail and then turned to reach up a large hand to assist Sibyl as she came down. Pale blond hairs glistened silvery in the sun on the back of the man's powerful hand.

Under his right arm, he carried the large package, or was it the same? Adria could have sworn the package was thicker, yes, it was, she was certain! What was in those packages? What business was Sibyl — and maybe even Larry — engaged in with this stranger?

It was very mysterious! To consider that mild, motherly Sibyl Graham could be involved with anything vicious was too ludicrous for words — absolutely absurd! Or something illegal? Not Sibyl! The thought was so ridiculous that she almost chuckled out loud.

And yet, what was she doing out here in the woods consorting with a man that might even be Kandy's assailant? What were they doing in the cave? What were they arguing about? That the argument had to do with both Larry and Kandy, she was almost certain. Hadn't she heard their names mentioned?

The man was now striding away up the trail, the large flat package still carried under his arm. The sun glittered on an object tucked into the man's belt at the back and Adria's heart seemed to suddenly be pumping ice water. The object was a pistol! She was certain of it. Her wide staring eyes swung back to Sibyl who remained standing in the path, watching the man as he moved away and then disappeared among the trees. Then Sibyl turned back and began a rapid descent down the trail. She passed close to Adria's hiding place and Adria held her breath in fear that she might be seen. Until she had time to ponder on what she had seen, Adria did not want her cousin to know she had spied upon her and the blond stranger.

But Sarah will tell her I've been up to the cave looking for her, Adria thought. Maybe I should just confront her. Not yet, she decided.

As silently as possible, she climbed down to a dim trail that Sibyl had passed; running down it for a short way, she took another path back to the house, arriving at the back gate before Sibyl.

Drawing in deep breaths she tried to still her panting before Sibyl came around the curving trail. When she heaved into sight, panting and red-faced, Adria strove to speak casually, "Hi! Are you getting your exercise? Where have you been?"

Sibyl stopped dead-still for a moment and stared at Adria and then came on down to stand beside her at the back gate. Her laugh was breathless — and distinctly forced — when she answered. "Yes, I went up in the trees for a stroll. It always relaxes me to walk in the woods. And goodness only knows, I needed it today!"

She stopped and peered at Adria, her china-blue eyes alert, "I thought you were going back to the hospital after you talked to that criminal at the jail."

"I did, but Kandy was still asleep and I

couldn't get Gentry to come out here to rest, so I came on out myself."

"You've been walking in the woods too?"

At Adria's non-committal nod, she asked almost too casually, "You didn't see anyone up there, did you? You know — someone suspicious looking."

"Oh, did you see someone suspicious looking?" Adria asked just as innocently. She hated to play this deceptive game but she needed to know, without lying to get information, if Sibyl was going to tell her about the strange man.

Sibyl locked eyes with her briefly and then turned quickly toward the house. "No, I saw no one. Come on in and let's have some lunch. I smell beef soup cooking and Sarah makes the best in the country."

As Adria followed her down the rough stone path toward the house, Sibyl said back over her shoulder, "How did it go with that Sam Tillet fellow? Do you think he was the one who shot Kandy?"

Adria had to pull her thoughts back to what Sibyl was saying. Her mind had been swirling with questions all the way down the path past the garden and now between the green, newly mown lawn.

Why had Sibyl lied about meeting with that blond stranger with the beard? Because it was quite obvious now that she had arranged to meet him up at the cave. What had been in that large, flat package?

And could that man be Kandy's assailant of two years ago and perhaps also be her shooter now? And if he was, what connection did he have with Kandy and Larry? And why had Larry so vigorously defended him against Kandy's accusation that he was her attacker? Did he have something on Larry, and Larry was afraid of him? She couldn't forget that Kandy and Gentry had both said he seemed "wiped out" after his argument with the man.

But maybe the man who had met Sibyl out near the cave wasn't the same person. There were many bearded men these days especially in the Taos area.

She realized suddenly that Sibyl had asked her a question and was now standing at the back steps, holding the door open for her with a question in her eyes.

"What did you say?" Adria asked. "I guess my mind was way off somewhere."

"I asked about your visit to the jail."

Adria moved up the steps past her into the house before she answered. Then she turned toward Sibyl and said slowly, "Sam says he didn't do it, and I'm inclined to believe him."

Sibyl stepped past her and headed toward the kitchen, "Let's just wash up in the kitchen." After they had washed their hands and were seated at the table with large bowls of Sarah's savory soup before them, Sibyl returned to her subject. "Tell me all about what the man said — everything."

As they ate, Adria related all of the interview except the part where Sam admitted he was her strange champion in Albuquerque and then had followed her around, even seeing her to bed at night. She couldn't have told why she omitted that part but told herself it wasn't important to the case at hand.

"If you don't think this Tillet man did the shooting, who do you think did?" Sibyl asked. "And why would anyone want to kill my sister?"

"Maybe it was that man Gentry and Kandy saw at Larry's shop. Kandy was certain he was her attacker."

But Sibyl was shaking her head, "No, I talked to Larry and he knows the man and is certain he would have no reason to harm Kandy, now or two years ago. What would be his motive? Kandy admits she never saw the man before."

"Except for the time he beat her?"

"But Larry was positive the man he knows

wasn't the person who attacked Kandy," Sibyl said.

"What motive does Sam have, for that matter?"

"Who knows!" Sibyl said. "There are perfectly normal looking people nowadays who do horrible acts of violence with seemingly no motive except maybe for a morbid 'high'."

"Gentry isn't convinced that Kandy's attack two years ago was a random mugging," Adria said slowly, "And he also thinks there was more to Larry and that bearded fellow's set-to than a little quarrel over a petty gambling debt."

Sibyl's eyes widened and she said sharply, "Does he have any proof of that?"

"N-no — but it seems to be a gut-feeling he has."

She leaned toward Sibyl, "Could the man have something on Larry and Larry is afraid of him? And maybe the man beat Kandy to make Larry do what he wanted him to do."

"Do you think Larry would actually have dealings with a man that would harm his sister?" Sibyl's voice was scornful. "Larry may not always be the strongest in character but he would turn a man over to the police as quick as the flick of a lamb's tail if he suspected he had harmed Kandy!"

"Perhaps — I hope so," Adria said. For a moment she stared at Sibyl, considering, and then she locked eyes with Sibyl and said clearly, "I saw you up at the cave with that bearded blond man, Sibyl. You were having an argument with him just like Larry was when Gentry and Kandy saw them together. He is the same man, isn't he?" she finished softly.

Chapter 20

As Sibyl stared at Adria her face reflected different emotions as they chased each other over her countenance, but anger, perhaps even fear, were the dominating emotions.

Her voice was taut with wrath and the haughty straightening of her plump shoulders and lifting of her round chin strengthened the impression. "Adria, I'm surprised at you! Spying on me, who has always tried to treat you just like I did my sister and brother! I'd be too ashamed to raise my head, if I were you!"

Adria felt hot blood rush into her face but she refused to be daunted by Sibyl's reproving words or stance. She raised her hand in a placating gesture but spoke firmly, "When Kandy's life is at stake I must do whatever I feel is necessary to find the gunman who tried to kill her. Unless he is apprehended, that ambusher will try again and will probably succeed the next time!"

For a moment Sibyl held her bulldog belligerence and then suddenly she wilted; her shoulders slumped, her face broke up and tears cascaded down her face. She covered her wet face with plump hands and her shoulders shook, although she uttered not a sound.

Adria got up and went around the table and bent to wrap her arms around Sibyl's shoulders. For a few moments Sibyl rested her hot wet face against Adria, her shoulders heaving. Adria said nothing, just held her — as Sibyl had so often held her, Larry and Kandy in their growing-up years.

"I-I'm sorry that I'm acting like such a baby. It must be that Kandy's getting shot has me completely unnerved."

Adria just patted her shoulders but remained silent.

Finally Sibyl lifted her head and Adria knelt to look into her red-blotched face tenderly, "I wasn't spying on you, Sibyl," she explained gently, "But Gentry said you seemed upset when you left the hospital and I thought I had better come see what was wrong. Sarah said you had gone up toward the cave so I went up there. When I saw you arguing with a tall, blond bearded stranger, I didn't know what to think, so I hid until you were both gone."

Sibyl stared into Adria's face for a moment, then self-consciously straightened up and reached for her glass of tea and drank thirstily. Setting it down she said with a slight tremor in her voice, "I don't know what you thought but one thing I'm confident of, Otto Colman did not harm Kandy."

Adria drew up a chair near Sibyl before she said in a puzzled voice, "But isn't he the man who was arguing with Larry?"

"Yes," Sibyl said, "but he is only a business associate of mine — and Larry's. Kandy is mistaken when she says he is the one who attacked her."

"But Kandy seemed so certain. She...."

"I know, she said his eyes betrayed his identity. But Kandy just has an overly active imagination." When Adria continued to look incredulous, Sibyl went on, "I have had business dealings with Otto for quite some time now and he has never been anything but kind and gentle and soft-spoken."

"But could not he have...."

"No, he wasn't the same man," Sibyl said adamantly. "Kandy said the man who beat her had close-clipped hair and wore no beard. I started doing business with Otto before her attack and Otto has always worn a beard and longish hair, sometimes shorter than other times but he has never been clean-shaven nor worn extremely short hair."

"There are wigs and false beards," Adria said hesitantly.

"Nonsense," Sibyl said decisively, "I approached him about it today and he assured me that Kandy was mistaken and I believe him."

Her kindly blue eyes held Adria's gray-blue ones in earnest entreaty, "Believe me, Adria, I know character and this man has never — ever — shown himself to be cruel and vicious as the man would have had to be to hurt and try to kill Kandy. He has always been honest and straight-forward with me. I've done business with him for better than two years so I should know him well by now."

"I hope you are right. . . ."

"I know I'm right. Otto didn't even get angry when I actually accused him of trying to hurt my sister. He was understanding and patient, just as he always is."

"I didn't know you were involved in any kind of business, Sibyl," Adria said, abruptly changing the subject. "You surprise me. What is the nature of your business?"

A slight pinkness appeared in Sibyl's cheeks and her eyes shifted briefly away from Adria's. "I-I . . ." she floundered to a stop and then said with a slight edge to her words, "My business is between Otto and me, and I would appreciate it if you didn't mention it to anyone, not even Kandy and Larry. It's strictly my own affair."

She leaned over and placed a warm, moist hand on Adria's arm, "Please promise me you won't tell anyone about this. After all, I am entitled to my privacy, am I not?"

When Adria continued to stare at Sibyl with troubled perplexed eyes, Sibyl said pleadingly, "What I am doing has nothing to do with Kandy but I do need your promise — at least for now — that you will tell no one of my involvement with Otto. Promise me, Adria!" she pressed.

"Very well, Sibyl, I promise." Adria could never withstand Sibyl's baby-blue eyes when they stared into hers that way.

But later after a brief rest, as she drove Sibyl back to the hospital, Adria still felt uneasy about Sibyl's connections with the man Kandy was so sure had hurt her. The fact that she wanted that connection kept secret also greatly disturbed her.

She breathed a silent prayer that God would help the police, or someone, to find the gunman who had lain in wait for Kandy, before he tried again to kill her.

Kandy was awake but very weak when Adria and Sibyl got to the hospital late that afternoon. But Gentry said excitedly that Kandy had eaten a little soft food and drank some fruit juice. Kandy's grin and whisper that they must not worry because God was watching out for her, brought tears to Sibyl's eyes and a bound of joy to Adria's heart.

In her fear for Kandy, Adria realized she had not relied on God as much as she should have. She must not forget that God was still the Lord of all, and that meant situations and circumstances too.

Adria was pleased when Gentry informed them that Larry had been in for a couple of quick visits during the day. Sometimes impulsive, good-looking Larry was not too responsible or as caring of others as he should be. It was common knowledge that he was derelict in his child-support payments for his six-year old daughter and she suspected he seldom visited her either. So it was a relief that he was concerned for Kandy.

He breezed in a few minutes after Adria and Sibyl arrived with a dewy bouquet of sweet-scented, deep-red rosebuds and planted a kiss on Kandy's forehead.

A nurse then came in and brusquely shooed them all out and took the flowers away to find a vase for them so she could add them to Gentry's huge living pot of flowers and Sibyl's bountiful bouquet of colorful blossoms from her own garden.

Mentally, Adria scolded herself for her own forgetfulness. Concern for Kandy's welfare had wiped all thoughts from her mind of pretty flowers or cards. I must remedy that, she thought guiltily.

Larry went back to his shop and Sibyl and Gentry moved together toward the waiting room. Adria called the police station to find out if there were any new developments in the shooting. Sam Tillet was still the only suspect, she was told. But there was one development. Sam Tillet had been released on a bail of two hundred thousand dollars. No, they did not know who had put up the money for his release.

The news shook Adria. Although she had assured Sibyl that she didn't think Sam was guilty of Kandy's attempted murder, it was alarming to have him free. What if he were guilty and just looking for another opportunity to kill Kandy. What was a judge thinking of to release the man!

Sam dressed in rather poor clothing, even his camping gear was well-worn. He certainly didn't appear affluent, yet he, or someone, had put up the required ten percent, or twenty thousand dollars, for his release. Who could have done that for this disturbed war veteran?

For the next three days, Adria found herself watching the streets and hospital corridors for Sam Tillet's tall, lanky figure but she saw him nowhere and his attorney didn't contact any of them.

Sibyl had called the judge who had set Sam free and demanded to know why he had released Sam when there was every evidence he had committed the shooting. The judge, who was a personal friend of Sibyl's father and well-known to her, admitted that he had not considered there was a chance Sam could come up with the bail money or he would have set it higher.

But he assured Sibyl that it was unlikely that even if Sam were Kandy's ambusher, that he would try again. "Sibyl," he soothed her, "he would know we would suspect him first and he would be slammed right back in jail. A guard has been stationed in the hall near Kandy's room."

On Sunday Adria went to church alone. Gentry still spent most of his time at the hospital. Kandy was much stronger now and her shoulder wound and head were healing nicely. Her excellent health was her best medicine, the doctor declared.

Although Kandy showed she appreciated the concern of her family it was plain that her greatest delight was in Gentry's company. Sometimes Adria would tiptoe in to find Gentry asleep in his chair and Kandy napping on the bed but with hands entwined and a happy smile on their lips.

I really should go home tomorrow, Adria thought, as she left the small church that she always attended with Kandy when she was in Taos. After all, she thought to herself with a smile, Kandy really doesn't see anyone else when Gentry is there.

Kandy's friends swarmed around Adria as she went out the church door, solicitous and caring as they always were. She knew the pastor and a couple of close friends had visited the hospital but most were waiting until Kandy was stronger to visit. But her church family sent their love and daily prayers, the pastor's young wife assured Adria.

Sibyl had convinced Gentry that he should come to lunch at The Lodge that day, with Kandy's full support. "That young man of yours is getting to be just a shadow," she informed Kandy. "He must come home and eat a decent meal."

With dancing eyes, Kandy told Gentry he might as well give in and he had reluctantly agreed to go.

Adria stopped in at the hospital before she went out to The Lodge for lunch. Sibyl and Gentry had just left. She found Kandy wan and pale but eating a light meal. But her dark eyes were shining like stars. As soon as Adria entered the room Kandy lifted her hand to show a magnificent diamond solitaire engagement ring. She agreed with Kandy that it was breathtakingly beautiful.

Adria stayed until Kandy finished her meal and then her guard dog nurse sent her away, insisting that Kandy needed her nap. As Adria went out the door of the hospital, she felt a wave of inexplicable desolation sweep over her. As she moved down the wide walk toward the parking lot her bewildered mind strove to understand her feelings.

Kandy was recovering and she and Gentry were so happy why was she, Kandy's cousin and closest friend, unhappy and depressed? It didn't make sense. Was she jealous of Kandy? Of course not, she told herself. Well, maybe she was a little envious. Not covetous of Kandy's joy, but sad for her own empty, raw heart. If only Giles would come back! But of course, he wasn't going to — not after all this time.

Her thoughts swung to Sam, the first man who had stirred even a flicker in her heart since Giles had jilted her. That was a one-way street too. The man was obviously disturbed and maybe even Kandy's attempted murderer. Life was the pits anyway!

After the delicious roast-beef lunch, Gentry — pressed by Sibyl — consented to rest a while before returning to Kandy. Sarah and Fritz always took a Sunday afternoon nap and so did Sibyl, but Adria was too restless to be confined in a room. She took Sarge and went up to the cave.

At the entrance she hesitated. The place was creepy to her since she had felt someone was watching her that time a while back. But Sibyl and Otto had spent some time there. Maybe she could find out more about this secret business of his and Sibyl's.

She pushed away the guilty feeling that Sibyl should have a right to her privacy. Yes, as long as it didn't mean danger to Kandy. And how would she know unless she looked into it?

Sarge pushed into the cave ahead of Adria and she was glad of his protection. Goose bumps rose on her arms as she entered the first room. This is as far as I plan to go, she thought.

She watched Sarge and he didn't seem disturbed so that must mean no one else was here. Adria let out the breath she had been holding and listened intently. No sound reached her ears and she felt better.

Her eyes drifted to Sarge again and her

heart began to pound. He was walking stiff-legged and warily to a large boulder that jutted partly out from the wall. The bristles stood up on his back and he growled low in his throat. His nose was touching the rock now and he growled again. It was all Adria could do to keep her feet from dashing toward the entrance.

Sarge was now sniffing along the floor at the base of the boulder and then up one side where it fit into the wall. Then he clawed vigorously at the rock on that side. Looking all around and listening until she felt her eardrums were bulging, Adria moved to Sarge's side. He looked up at her and whined, then clawed again at the rock.

Adria turned on her flashlight as the room was only dimly lighted by the crack high up, near the ceiling. Coming close to the wall, she studied the rock from every angle. Sarge was again clawing at the rock at one side. She moved to examine that side more closely. Running her fingers along the edge at the side, she found a definite indentation at one place about hip high. Placing her finger under the lip, she pulled out. For a moment nothing happened and then slowly the boulder moved under her fingers. Adria was so startled that she jumped back. The blood in her veins was now pounding wildly and it felt like the hair on her head was literally standing up. This sort of thing happened only in novels and movies!

Looking around to see that no one was watching her actions, Adria again pulled out on the handle-like recess and again the boulder moved. As she continued to pull, the rock rolled outward until it rested against the wall. Beyond was a low doorway in the rock.

With fast-beating heart, she bent down and flashed her light into the opening beyond. A small room came into view. Her legs felt weak and trembly with excitement and fear but she drew in her breath and ducked low so she could enter.

On the other side of the opening she gingerly stood up and flashed her light about. The room was clearly not a natural cave, but had been drilled and blasted so the sides were fairly straight and the ceiling was perhaps six and a half feet high. It was floored with smooth flat rocks put together with a mortar of some sort. She saw immediately that all the work was very old. Had this been a hideout for stolen goods or bootleg whiskey sometime in the past?

The first thing that her eyes lit upon was the camping equipment that she had found in the inner cave room. She walked over to examine it, piled in one corner, and saw that it all seemed to be there, except the three guns and ammunition. Even the wicked-looking knife was there.

A strong odor of cigar smoke assailed her nostrils. She wondered if that was what Sarge had smelled that led to his interest in the rock opening which his nose told him must be here.

Sarge was sniffing at a large paper-wrapped package that stood against the wall. Adria quickly moved to look and her heart missed a beat. It looked like the package that Otto had been carrying when Sibyl had met him!

About twenty-four by thirty-six inches, or perhaps a little more, the flat package was wrapped in heavy oiled paper and taped with heavy strapping tape. Adria felt of it and decided it must be a picture, or painting, in a frame. But what was a picture doing here — obviously hidden?

Going back to the camping gear, Adria took up the knife. She hated to snoop but she needed to know what was going on here. Sibyl would hate her if she found her here! She must hurry.

Carefully Adria slit the tape on one end of the package and working carefully, she soon was able to put her hand on the end of the frame and pull it out of the wrapping, leaving the wrapping whole on three sides.

Another wrapping covered the object, of cloth, this time. Only a few pieces of tape held it together and it took only a minute to bring the painting to light.

And a breathtaking painting it was, of a winter scene so realistic that she could almost feel the cold of the ice on the river and the warmth from the one lighted window of the small cabin in the picture. Even in the limited light of her flashlight, she could see the skillfulness of the shading. A master had done this painting!

She turned the picture so she could read the small lettering in the corner and gasped. No wonder the landscape appeared to be done by a master painter. It was! The man's identification in the corner was of a famous artist that even she knew about with her limited knowledge of painting and artists.

A terrible dread compressed her chest and made it difficult for her to breathe. Was Sibyl engaged in helping to steal and sell valuable paintings? It seemed too incredible for her mind to take in.

Dazedly she slipped the painting back into the cloth wrapping and pressed the tape back on as well as she could. Then she replaced it in the outer wrapping and folded down the cut edges and set it once more in the rack it had come from. The thief would know it had been tampered with but there was no helping that now.

Sarge suddenly moved toward the door, whining softly. She heard the rattle of steps on the gravelly shelf outside the cave entrance. Someone was coming!

Terror struck her under the ribs like a saber and it sent her rushing across the floor and out the opening. Sarge plunged ahead of her. Once out, she hastily tugged at the rock door. It was not fully back in place when she heard swift, heavy steps in the entrance and heard labored breathing. Someone was in the room with them! She pushed the rock back into place and turned swiftly to face the intruder, her own breath coming in gasps.

Sibyl was standing just inside the entrance!

Chapter 21

Sibyl stood in the entrance way. Her face was red and damp with perspiration. Her blue eyes were wide and fear-filled as she stared at Adria. She was panting from the climb up the hill.

They stared at each other and Adria felt guilty red flood into her face. Sibyl took a step toward her and Adria shrank back. Her voice sounded squeaky as she spoke. "Sibyl, I-I. . . ."

Sibyl's eyes were cold and unfriendly when she interrupted. "Always the snooping reporter. You just wouldn't let this alone, would you?"

"I had to know," Adria said miserably. "But I never dreamed I would find out your 'business' with Otto would be stealing valuable paintings!"

Sibyl flinched as if Adria had struck her, her voice now held an uncertain note, "It isn't what it seems!"

Adria stood away from the wall and took a step toward Sibyl, "What is it then, Sibyl?"

Sarge was pushing his head against Sibyl's stout body and she thrust him angrily away. "Call this stupid dog off of me."

Adria called the dog to her side and then asked, "What is going on, Sibyl?"

"I guess you'll rush right to the police," Sibyl said in a choking voice.

Adria felt a rush of sympathy toward her cousin. "Sibyl, what have you gotten yourself into?"

Sibyl swallowed hard and then reiterated, "It isn't what it seems."

Adria touched Sibyl's arm and spoke gently, "Come sit down and tell me about it. Maybe I can help."

"I-I'm not sure anyone can," Sibyl said in a subdued voice and allowed herself to be led across the cave-room. At Adria's command Sarge lay down at her feet after she had seated Sibyl in an aluminum chair that was kept folded against a wall. Unfolding its mate and seating herself across from her, Adria said gently, "Now, tell me, please. What is that valuable painting doing here?"

Tears filled Sibyl's eyes and ran down her plump cheeks. She rubbed them away on the sleeve of the old gardening shirt she wore. "It didn't seem so wrong when I first came up with the idea."

"What idea?" Adria prompted gently.

Sibyl mopped her face again with her sleeve. Leaning toward Adria, she said earnestly, "You know how Larry has failed at

234

the things he has tried and when he came up with the idea of the gift shop, Father absolutely refused to finance another venture."

"Yes, I know about that," Adria said.

"The gift shop seemed like something that would really work for Larry and I pled with Father to help Larry but he refused. Larry was desperate. His credit isn't good so he couldn't borrow the money to get started from anyone."

"So you came up with an idea to get it for Larry?"

"Yes, and it worked!" Sibyl's eyes took on a soft glow of pride. "I have never seen Larry so happy and the shop is doing really well."

Her words became a plea, "You won't take away his chance, will you, Adria? Please say you will not tell the police about this. Please!"

"I don't know yet what you did," Adria said.

"Oh yes — I guess I didn't tell you. You see, I used to go to the courthouse to hear some of Father's cases. I was so proud of Father! He nearly always won his cases. He could just spellbind the jurors! Did you ever hear him, Adria?"

"A couple of times. He was good."

"Yes, he was. But that time he lost the

case, the man was released on a techni-cality."

"Was the man Otto Colman?"

"Yes — Otto was charged with stealing valuables from wealthy homes when they were away on vacation. He wouldn't have been caught that time but the family came back sooner than expected."

"Then the man you are doing business with is a criminal?"

"In a way," Sibyl admitted. "Anyway, I contacted him and told him a plan that I came up with while the trial was going on. He would steal valuable paintings and I would reproduce them. Then he would return the paintings before the owner re-turned from vacation. Is that so bad? We re-turned the painting each time."

"You have been reproducing the work of famous artists?" Adria asked in astonish-ment.

"Yes," Sibyl said proudly, "And they can scarcely be told from the originals!"

"Then you could have done fine work on your own and sold it! Why did you feel you had to reproduce other people's work?"

"I'm an unknown," Sibyl said. "It takes time to gain recognition and sometimes the breaks never do come your way. Larry needed money then, not ten years from then."

"How many paintings have you reproduced?"

"Twenty, Otto sells them and we half the money."

"And you made enough to set Larry up in business that way?"

"Yes, the paintings have brought an amazing amount of money," Sibyl said.

"And I suppose you used the secret room for a trysting place."

"Yes, Otto would leave me a painting and I would reproduce it and bring them both back here for him to pick up. We seldom even saw each other."

"How did you know about this room?"

Sibyl chuckled, "You forget that I have lived at The Lodge for many years more than any of you. It belonged to my mother's family and Mother showed me the room. Her father had made it to hide some kind of contraband, she would never tell me what. Even Father never knew about it."

She sighed, "I guess I never told anyone because it was my very own secret place where I could come and bring back the memory of my dear mother."

"Does Larry know you and Otto stole and reproduced famous paintings?"

"No, and you mustn't tell him! If I go to jail I don't want him implicated."

"How did you loan him the money without him finding out what you had done?"

"Otto took care of that too. He told Larry he had heard he needed a backer and he was willing to loan him the money. The money was my cut, of course. And Larry has made every payment with interest," she finished proudly.

Adria's mind was reeling. Sibyl, a law-breaker? It was unbelievable! "Sibyl, don't you realize that you have not only broken the law yourself but you have drawn Otto back into crime too. And who would ever believe that Larry is not in on this."

Sibyl's lips trembled and she placed a hand over them to still their quivering. "I-I really never meant to break the law, Adria. I was just so desperate for Larry." Her eyes filled with tears. "Larry has always seemed like a little boy to me — my little boy, be-cause my stepmother was never well and I always cared for him. Don't you see why I had to help him?"

When Adria only looked at her helplessly, she rushed on, "Larry might have turned to drink for consolation! He's given to that you know. And Larry is a good boy, even if he isn't always so — so responsible."

"You said you managed to get Larry set

up long ago. Why have you and Otto continued in this — this business?"

Sibyl looked down at her plump hands that she was twisting together, "I wanted to quit as soon as we had enough to set Larry up but Otto has kept bringing me paintings to reproduce, not as many as at first but one now and then."

She looked up at Adria, her face tense and strained, "I had it out with Otto yesterday. I told him I would do no more paintings after I did the one he had just brought me."

"Did he agree to that?"

"Yes, he said he was getting a little worried too. That we had a good run and we shouldn't be greedy. After this one we are quitting for good, Adria. I promise."

"And you think Otto will let you quit?"

"Yes, of course! He was very agreeable, he always is."

"He has never threatened you or hurt you in any way?"

"Of course not! He is the perfect gentleman, always has been! That's why I know he could never have harmed Kandy."

"I think you should return this painting and not do another one," Adria said firmly. "And you know you must tell the police what you have done, don't you?"

Horror filled Sibyl's eyes. "But it would

kill Father, and Kandy and Larry if they knew I had broken the law! And it wouldn't be fair to Otto! Please, Adria, promise you won't tell anyone about this."

When Adria remained silent, tears again began to run down her cousin's pink cheeks. "At least give me a little time to get used to the idea of maybe going to jail."

Her shoulders began to shake with violent sobs and she buried her face in her hands.

Adria knelt down and drew Sibyl's head to her shoulder and held her. "I promise to not do anything right now, Sibyl. Please don't cry. Just think this over and I believe you will agree with me what you will have to do."

After a few moments, Sibyl's sobs subsided and she lifted a tear-blotched face. "T-thank you, Adria. I imagine you are right, but give me a day or so to get my thinking straight. Okay?" Her attempt at a smile was wavery.

"That's more like my dear cousin," Adria said gently as she hugged her and planted a kiss on her hot forehead. "Remember, I will back you and support you every step of the way. And I'm sure Kandy and Larry will too."

"But what about Father? All his life he has been on the right side of the law. Before he became District Attorney he would never take the case of someone he knew was guilty. And now his own daughter has broken the law."

She was beginning to cry again and Adria intervened quickly, "Why should he even know? He scarcely knows what is going on anyway. We don't have to tell him!"

"You're right!" Sibyl's face cleared. "We'll protect him from this disgrace!"

She struggled to her feet. "We must go now. It will be time to go to the hospital soon; Gentry has already gone." Her face clouded, "Oh, I do hope this will not hurt Kandy's relationship with Gentry!" She turned a tragic face to Adria, "Maybe Gentry won't marry the sister of a jailbird!"

"I don't believe Gentry would let that stand in his way, not if he really loves Kandy, and I'm sure he does. Besides, you aren't in jail yet," Adria said. "You did wrong but let's just pray and leave the results with God."

"I'm not sure God will want any part of me either," Sibyl said tragically.

"Nonsense! He loves you regardless of what you did." Adria reached out to touch Sibyl's face with a tender hand, "This would be a good time to take God on as your special friend, Sibyl. He is waiting with outstretched arms anytime you are willing to receive Him."

Adria held her breath. She had spoken to Sibyl only once about accepting Jesus Christ as Savior and Sibyl had replied virtuously that she lived a better life than most so-called Christians.

"You think Jesus would want me now? After what I have done?" Sibyl asked incredulously.

"I'm sure He would!"

Hope flared brightly in Sibyl's eyes for a moment and then dimmed. "I'll have to think about this for a bit. Maybe later." She turned away and started toward the cave entrance.

"Don't wait too long, Sibyl," Adria said softly. "None of us are promised another day."

But Sibyl stooped to pass from sight through the cave exit.

Adria followed, Sarge beside her. "Let me go down first and I'll give you a hand," Adria said as she started down the steep incline. Suddenly she stopped. Sarge had bounded down to a little bench about a foot wide and was sniffing at something. Adria skidded on down to stand just above him.

Clearly imprinted in the dust was a partial footprint, with a leaf pattern. The print was new, made after she and Sibyl had gone up to the cave. She was sure because the print partly obliterated one of Sibyl's and two of her own. Someone had been up to the cave while she and Sibyl were in there!

A chill traveled down Adria's back as she scanned the whole area with wide eyes. Sibyl had scrambled down to stand near her. "What's wrong, Adria," she asked.

Adria pointed at the clear print in the dust, "Is that Otto Colman's footprint?"

Sibyl bent to look and almost skidded off her perch on the rough, steep incline. Adria reached a hand to steady her. Sibyl sat down on a rock and again bent to examine the print. "I don't know, why?"

Adria spoke softly, "That print was not there when you and I climbed up to the cave. See how it partially covers my athletic shoe print and yours."

Sibyl stared for a moment and then lifted her head to look about them. When she spoke her voice was almost a whisper. "You think that was Otto and he heard what I told you?"

"Sam said the man he saw near the cave recently wore a hiking boot with a leaf-pattern on the sole. He saw his tracks."

"Otto does wear hiking boots," Sibyl said thoughtfully. "If Otto heard me telling you about our business he will be angry.

"Of course it might not be Otto's," she continued, "but there is a good chance it is. It's very seldom anyone trespasses on our land."

"I think we had better get back to the house," Adria said quickly. Alarm was ringing loudly in her innermost being.

Without a word, Sibyl started down the trail. Adria called Sarge to them and followed. As they descended, Adria raked the slopes with her eyes but saw no one. However, she knew there was little likelihood that she would with so many places to hide.

As they quickly moved down the hillside, Adria pondered. If the footprint belonged to Otto and he now knew Sibyl had told her about the theft of the paintings, what would Otto do? Was he really the mild, kind man that Sibyl and Larry believed him to be, or was he the man who had attacked Kandy. And even if he was not Kandy's assailant, the man might be dangerous if he felt threatened because Adria knew of his thefts.

Adria was glad when they were off the trail and inside the house. While she showered and got ready to go to the hospital, she tried to decide what to do. If only she had someone to talk with about this! Then she chided herself. She did have someone!

And she did talk to that person immediately. After a good talk with God, she felt much better and determined to put the whole mess in God's hands. Certainly she didn't know how to handle any of this and God did, so she would just give it to Him.

She and Sibyl arrived at the hospital to receive very good news. If Kandy continued to improve she would be home in two or three days.

Chapter 22

All the next morning Adria pondered if she should go home to Albuquerque. Kandy was rapidly getting better. When she and Sibyl arrived that morning, Kandy told them ecstatically that she had even been for a short walk down the hall with Gentry's help, and had eaten a "logger-sized breakfast". But when Adria mentioned she might go home, Kandy pled with her to stay at least a couple of more days.

On the way into town, Adria had asked Sibyl what she intended doing about the "business" she and Otto were engaged in and Sibyl had answered vaguely, "I want to wait until Kandy is home before I do anything. Nothing must upset Kandy right now."

"I'm still uneasy about that footprint we found," Adria told her. "What if it was Otto's and . . . ?"

Sibyl broke in impatiently, "Otto wouldn't like it but I'm sure he would be reasonable. He always has been."

"But if you disclose your part in that scheme his part will automatically come out," Adria argued.

"I'm not sure what I will do," Sibyl said without looking at Adria, "but I mustn't divulge Otto's involvement. It wouldn't be fair to him. After all it was my idea, not his."

"He's a grown man," Adria said a bit tartly. "He didn't have to go along with it."

"I'm sorry but I can't do that to Otto," Sibyl said with asperity.

"Are you in love with this Otto guy?" Adria spouted out the words before she had time to think them through.

She slanted a look at Sibyl and saw her plump cheeks take on a slightly rosy tinge. "You do care about him!"

Sibyl dropped her eyes to her hands twisting in her ample lap and spoke so low Adria could scarcely hear, "I know a handsome man like Otto would never give me a second glance if it were not for our partnership. But yes," her words were defiant, "I do care for him — very much!"

Adria sat stunned. Of course Sibyl could fall in love with a man, it was only natural, but Adria had never thought of Sibyl as anything but a comfortable motherly woman who lavished care and love on them all. Why should she not want the love of a man?

She thought of Larry's denunciation of his father, blaming him for never allowing Sibyl to have a life of her own. Perhaps we are all guilty, she thought. Depending on her and expecting her to be there when we needed her. And now she has fallen for a criminal! But — perhaps he is what Sibyl believes him. I certainly hope so, she thought despondently. Sibyl deserves the best.

She reached over and squeezed Sibyl's hand, "You are young, yet, Sibyl. Even if this romance doesn't work out, there are other men who are looking for the kind of woman you are. You just need to break loose from the ties of home and go out among other people. There's someone out there who will be perfect for you."

"Oh, sure! If I go to jail maybe I will meet the right man there," Sibyl said with a cynical laugh. And she clammed up and could not be drawn into conversation the rest of the drive to the hospital.

Later, after they came home from the hospital, Adria and Sibyl were preparing a light lunch when Sarah called Adria to the telephone.

A brisk young woman's voice spoke in Adria's ear, "This is Lori down at Blue Corn Treasures. Larry asked me to call and have you and Sibyl meet him at the cave at twelve-thirty. He will go up the trail from the road, he said, and that you would know what he meant."

"What is this all about?" asked Adria.

"I really don't know, except your cousin said he has found out something very interesting that he wants you and Sibyl to see. He asked that you don't bring anyone else with you or tell anyone else. Larry asked me to call from a public phone while I'm on my break."

Lori laughed, "This is very mysterious, isn't it? Larry left in his car a few minutes ago like demons were on his trail."

When Adria told Sibyl about the message, Sibyl looked thoughtful. "Maybe we should call the shop and see if that was really one of his salesgirls."

Adria did, and a different voice came on the line after three rings. "Could I speak to Larry," Adria asked.

"I'm sorry but Larry left just a few minutes ago. Didn't say where he was going or when he was coming back."

"Is Lori there?"

"No, she's on her break, left about the same time Larry did."

"Did you happen to hear Larry telling Lori to call us?"

"No, but now that I think of it, Lori did go into Larry's office for a couple of minutes right before she went to lunch."

Adria had held the receiver so Sibyl could hear too, so when Adria hung up, her cousin said anxiously, "Do you suppose Larry found out about the paintings?"

"I don't know but I guess we will know soon enough."

"Let me slip into some pants," Sibyl said hurriedly, looking at her watch. "It's already ten after twelve."

As they went out the door, Adria whistled for Sarge and he came bounding up. "Do we have to take that animal?" Sibyl asked.

For a moment Adria hesitated. "If it's all right with you, I think we should take him for protection."

Sibyl acquiesced reluctantly.

When they came to the foot of the incline that led to the cave entrance, Adria swept the ground with her eye and saw no alarming footprints. She admitted to herself that she was looking for the leaf pattern footprint.

They quickly climbed to the entrance and after surveying the area about them, Adria stooped and followed Sibyl. Sarge, who had bounded down the trail, had come rushing back at Adria's call and entered just ahead of Adria. Suddenly he stopped and growled low in his throat. Sibyl was already through the entrance and had stepped aside to admit Adria and Sarge.

Adria, alarmed, stopped and began to back out of the cave. At the same time that Sarge growled, Adria saw a fresh footprint with a leaf design in the soft dirt just ahead of her, illuminated by a light inside. But at that instant a man's voice spoke, "Come right on in, Miss Adria. I have a gun leveled right at your cousin's head."

An icy chill swept over Adria and she stopped backing abruptly. Her head was ducked under the low ceiling of the entrance way and she was unable to see into the room. Sarge was moving stiff-legged into the room and at a reiteration of the deep voiced command, Adria stepped in after him and stood up. The pungent odor of cigar smoke permeated the air.

She laid a hand on Sarge's head and looked around. In the bright glare of two lighted butane lanterns, Adria saw standing across the room a tall man with pale hair and a full beard. A small brown cigar lay smoking on a slightly jutting rock at his elbow. His body, encased in expensive-looking dark trousers and a short sleeved knit shirt made her think of a mountain lion, muscular and lithe as he shifted his body with easy grace to face them. On his feet were black hiking boots.

The man's bare arms rippled with steel-like muscles and his hand held a .357 Magnum. Tucked into a carved leather holster on a heavy belt at his waist was a .38 police revolver. Two of the guns Adria had seen in the inner cave-room!

Sarge was quivering at Adria's side and the man said harshly, "I would restrain that animal, if I were you. It would set back Kandy's recovery tragically if she should lose him by a well-placed bullet."

Adria spoke softly to Sarge, ordering him to sit and he instantly complied, though he kept his dark eyes fixed upon the man with the gun.

Sibyl spoke at her side and Adria turned to glance at her. Sibyl's eyes were wide and staring, her face pasty, lips trembling. "Otto, what are you doing with that gun?"

Otto's eyes were blue ice as they swung to Sibyl, his deep voice deadly, "I'll use this if I have to, Sibyl dear." His sculptured lips curled with scorn as he said softly, "I should kill you anyway for spilling everything you know!"

Sibyl lifted a plump placating hand, "Otto, I would never have implicated you. I-I told Adria so." She licked her pale lips nervously before rushing on, "And I tried to get you on the phone to tell you Adria had discovered the painting but you were out. I would never betray you. You must believe me."

"Quiet!" Otto's voice cracked like a whip-lash in the echoing cave. His pale blue eyes were staring beyond Adria's back. He lowered his voice and motioned, "Move together, over there, the dog too. If either of you breathe a word it will be your last!"

Adria heard it then, a slight rattle of pebbles and the crunch of feet on gravel. Sarge leaned forward and whined softly. Adria laid her hand on Sarge's head when Otto bent a vicious look on the dog.

"Adria, Sibyl, are you in there?" The voice was Larry's.

"You," Otto pointed the gun at Adria. "Call to him, and act like nothing is wrong or I'll drill a hole in Sibyl's heart." His whispered command was laden with menace.

"In here," Adria heard herself calling, surprised that her voice did not tremble with the fear that was beating in her throat.

There was a quick shuffle of feet and Larry's head appeared in the doorway. He stepped into the room and stood up. His mouth fell open and he stammered, "H-hey — what's going on here?"

His quick glance took in Adria, Sibyl and Sarge to his left and then swung back to the gun in Otto's large muscular hand. "What's the big idea, Otto? Is this some kind of joke?" An uncertain grin tugged at the corners of his lips.

But the fierce light that suddenly leaped into the pale, icy blue eyes of the blond man and his ugly chuckle instantly erased the grin from Larry's lips and an angry frown appeared, "Put that gun down, Otto, before you hurt someone."

"Get over there with the others, spread out a little so I can watch you all," Otto commanded. When Larry didn't move, he lashed out, "Perhaps you would like to see blood running out of that silly sister of yours. Move!"

Larry moved quickly to stand near the others but his face now was dark with anger, "Tell me what this is all about!"

The lithe figure moved slightly, leveling the gun right at Larry's chest and his left hand moved to caress the butte of the gun in the holster at his side. "One more guest has been invited to our little party — and he's the guest of honor — so we will wait on him. Now, I want every mouth sealed until I say so!"

Adria saw Larry's mouth begin to open and then he clamped it closed again as Otto shifted ever so slightly and that strange fire leaped into his eyes again. Adria knew now without a shadow of a doubt that this man was the one who had beaten Kandy a couple of years before, and also had shot her. Why? her mind shrieked. But she dared not voice it. That this man was a cold-blooded killer she now knew with deadly certainty.

Sarge was sitting close beside her, she noticed. If she gave him the signal, could he rush Otto and disarm him before he hurt or killed someone? She measured the distance across the room with her eyes with sinking heart. She would only get Kandy's dog killed and maybe someone else as well.

She looked up and saw Otto's bleak eyes studying her.

"Don't try it, little Miss Reporter," the command was soft but its menace cut to the bone. A shudder swept through her and mocking appeared in the frigid depths of his eyes. "That's right, I wouldn't hesitate to mow you all down; it would be my pleasure, in fact."

His chuckle chilled Adria clear to her toes. We aren't coming out of this alive, she thought. Otto couldn't afford to let any of us live! But what was his plan? Who else had been tricked into coming to take part in this deadly tryst?

Dear God, the prayer rose up unbidden from her innermost being. "You alone can stop this madman. Don't let us die. Larry and Sibyl do not even know you. Dear Jesus, save us and give them another chance to come to you."

Sarge suddenly sat up straighter and turned his head toward the entrance way. A soft whine came from his jaws and Adria whispered for him to be still.

"Not a word out of anyone!" The cruel lips twisted and that terrifying light flared in his eyes, "Our last guest is arriving and we don't want to spoil his surprise!"

Suddenly a voice spoke outside and Adria jumped. "Adria! Are you in the cave?"

It was Sam Tillet's voice.

Chapter 23

"Answer Sam," Otto commanded, "And remember, I could wipe you all out before any of you could take two steps."

With a sinking heart Adria did as she was told.

Sam moved into the room and took in the scene with a slow, measured stare. He still wore his dark glasses. His eyes swung back to Otto, who held the gun ready, a cold grin on his face.

"Don't move a muscle or this pretty little Adria gal is dead meat," Otto snarled.

The deep silence in the room seemed to pound on Adria's eardrums and her nerves stretched achingly tight.

Suddenly Adria knew Sam was going to rush Otto and it was suicide, she knew. Otto's gun was pointed right at his chest. Perhaps it was in the slight tightening she saw in his jaw and the tensing, she more felt than saw, of his wiry body. Was that "berserk demon" taking control of his reason again?

Her voice was loud in the echoing cave, "Sam! Sam!" Finally she had his attention and Sam's head was turning toward her slowly, "How did this maniac get you to come out here?" She tried to keep her voice loud but calm. "Otto had someone call to tell us that Larry wanted us to meet him in the cave. Is that how he got you here too?"

Adria felt the tension easing in Sam's body as he stood silent for a second, shook his head as if to clear it, and then said quite lucidly, "A lady called me too. Said she was a nurse at the hospital and that you had left a message for me to meet you out here."

Otto stood silent, a smirk on his handsome face but his gun hand never wavered.

"A girl called at my gift shop too," Larry said angrily, "and left a message with one of my salesgirls. Said she was Adria and for me to meet her out here. Like a fool, I never thought to question it."

Now Otto's cold voice cut through the echoing room like a sharp blade, "We've had our little reunion and now it's time to get down to business."

"What is this all about?" Sam asked in a calm, almost conversational, voice.

"I'll ask the questions," Otto said with a slight swagger. Adria sensed that this killer loved the power he wielded over his victims. Was that why that wild savage fire leaped into his eyes whenever violence was even hinted at?

"Why did you beat Kandy?" Adria demanded.

Otto's cold gaze swung to lock with Adria's and she felt as if she were drowning in the terrifying blue fire in his eyes. No wonder Kandy remembered his eyes. They were paralyzing — like a cobra's pinned on a trapped victim!

His laugh was chilling as he answered, "I didn't even know Kandy but I had to put some teeth in a bargain I was trying to strike with big brother Larry, here." His eyes swung like a hawk's to rake over Larry and then back to Adria.

She strove to stare into his eyes but her stomach suddenly knotted in painful knots and she dropped her eyes to her trembling hands.

Otto's harsh laugh held victorious mockery.

Suddenly Sibyl's voice, almost a bleat, rang shrill in the cave, "What kind of deal did you make with Larry? You were suppose to only put up the money for Larry's gift shop and that was all!"

"Dear ignorant, trusting Sibyl," Otto favored her with a look of withering scorn, "You didn't think I would stop at pennies when I could make really big bucks, did you?"

"What did you do?" Sibyl asked almost humbly.

"He made me launder money for his criminal connections!" Larry said explosively. A shudder ran over his tall body as he looked beseechingly at Sibyl, "Believe me, Sibyl, I didn't want to do it but he had hurt Kandy badly once and threatened to kill her the next time.

"And like the fool that I seem to be, I believed him when he said he would never harm her again if I did what he asked!"

"That's what the argument was about that Kandy and Gentry saw you and Otto having, wasn't it?" Adria asked. If only we can keep him talking perhaps help will come or an opportunity to escape will present itself, she was thinking desperately.

"Yes, Otto had promised I would only have to launder his money for a year, but that morning he was insisting on me continuing for another year." He looked at Otto with angry, condemning eyes, "And I believed you when you called me after Kandy and Gentry were gone and said you had changed your mind and I would no longer have to launder that dirty money anymore!"

Otto's chuckle was chilling, "Kandy recognized me so I decided to cut loose from all of you as quickly as possible."

"You were the one who shot Kandy," Sam more stated than asked.

"Sure!" The thin cruel lips seemed to savor the flavor of his words, "The little fool would have been safe if she hadn't showed so plain that she knew me. I had to get rid of her before she started the police to asking questions."

"And I suppose you will try to finish her off yet," Adria heard herself saying bitterly.

"No, I'm setting up a situation where I will no longer be implicated," Otto said smugly. "Then I can go my merry way with no hint of suspicion linked to me."

"You are a despicable man," Sibyl said through pinched lips.

Larry suddenly turned suspicious dark eyes upon Sibyl, "How did you know Otto had put up the money for my gift shop?"

When Sibyl was silent, twisting her fingers together nervously, Otto spoke tauntingly, "You will be pleased to know that your respectable big sister — daughter of your highly respectable lawyer father — painted copies of famous paintings that I stole for her from wealthy homes!"

The color drained from Larry's face and he said in a choking voice, "I-I don't believe it!"

"Sure she did!" Otto gloated. "And I sold them for her and we split the money, pretty lucrative. But don't be so goody goody, my respectable shop-owner, your shop was purchased with your big sister's half of our illicit operation!"

"I did it for you," Sibyl said, turning anguished eyes upon Larry. "You desperately needed money and I got it the only way I could come up with."

Larry moved over to slip an arm about Sibyl and said huskily, "You are the greatest sister a guy ever had. I'll make you proud of me yet, I promise!"

"That will be a hard promise to keep," Sam said bitingly. "I don't think our gun-happy friend here has plans for anyone to leave this room alive."

"That's a smart man," Otto said with a cynical chuckle. "You see," he tilted his head to one side and smirked, "Sergeant Tillet, here, suffered such harrowing experiences in combat and in a prison camp that he has these 'spells' where he thinks everyone is the enemy creeping up on him."

Adria saw the red flood beginning to darken Sam's face and the tensing of his muscles. Otto's gun had tipped down slightly as if his gunhand was becoming weary. If Sam attacked Otto would he have a chance? I doubt it, she thought despairingly.

Otto shifted his lithe body and brought the gun up level again, scornful eyes raking his captive audience as he continued his mocking harangue. "No one will believe Sam's mind didn't flip out and plan this diabolical little scheme and leave you all to die in this tomb-like cave."

"And then what will happen to me?" Sam asked sarcastically. "After you've wiped out two entirely helpless women — like the coward you are — and blown away a young man in the prime of life, I suppose you will execute me! Big brave man!" His tone dripped scorn and loathing.

A red mantle rushed into Otto's face and his teeth grated together in rage, as he tightened his hold upon the gun in his big hand, "Maybe I'll keep you for a bit and make you beg for mercy."

"Go ahead and shoot, you sniveling coward," Sam goaded. "I've faced your kind of scum before! Give you a gun and you're a big bragging bully but without one you would run like a scared jackrabbit!"

The red in Otto's face drained away, leaving it a pasty white. His eyes blazed in insane fury and then the gun exploded in his hand. At the same instant, Sam leaped sideways, away from the others, and came up in a crouch. The roar of the gun was deafening in the cave.

Otto's lips were drawn back from his teeth in a wolfish snarl as he once again pointed the gun at Sam. Instantly Sam, who had narrowed the gap between himself and Otto, launched himself like a projectile directly at Otto and the gun.

The roar of the gun was shattering in the close confines of the cave. Adria saw with horror the flinch of Sam's body as the bullet tore into his body. He hesitated only a split second but the gun spat again and Adria heard the bullet whistle and then felt the spatter of rock splinters when it hit the rock wall behind her. She saw a red stain appear high on Sam's right shoulder and then scarlet trickling down his back.

Sam was grappling with Otto now, his long fingers gripping his wrist that held the gun. Adria was suddenly aware of Sarge, trembling under her restraining hand. Adria gave him the command to attack and disarm.

With a savage snarl, Sarge leaped forward. And it was not too soon, Adria saw that Sam's arm was trembling with the effort to hang onto Otto's powerful gun hand. Sarge jumped up and fastened his teeth in Otto's arm just below Sam's hand. Otto let out a shriek. Sarge's weight pulled the two struggling figures to the ground.

Everything had happened so fast that the others had stood by in stunned silence. Now Larry sprang to help Sam, first grabbing the gun from Otto's now writhing, limp fingers. Adria ran forward to take it and backed out of the way. Otto, broad of shoulder and powerful of torso, fought like the snarling mountain lion he reminded Adria of. Sarge's awesome snarls ripped the air.

Sarge now saw that Otto no longer had a weapon and he dropped the bloodied arm and leaped for his throat, growling savagely. Otto swore and tried to keep the gleaming teeth away with an up flung arm but the dog burrowed in, teeth snapping angrily. Otto rolled away from the gleaming teeth, trying to protect his head and throat with his arms. The arm Sarge had initially seized was torn and dripped blood.

Sam had fallen back now, his face white and contorted with pain, but Larry took his place — a place that no longer needed filled, however, for Otto was now pleading desperately with them to call the dog off of him.

Larry stood up and said savagely, "Maybe I should just let Sarge tear your throat out, you dirty killer!"

But Sibyl spoke from where she was huddled near the wall. "Don't let Sarge kill him,

Larry. There's been enough hurt already."

Adria handed the Magnum she had retrieved to Larry and commanded Sarge to let Otto up. Sarge backed off from the man but stood close, teeth bared and tongue dripping pink-tinged saliva.

"Sibyl, do you know where some rope is?" Larry asked. He had drawn out Otto's other gun and handed it to Adria. Now he quickly ran his hand over Otto's body and brought a razor-sharp knife from a sheath at the back of his belt. All the time, Larry had the .357 pressed into Otto's back.

Sibyl moved quickly to the door in the wall and was tugging it open while Adria stooped over Sam. When he saw that Sarge and Larry had Otto under control, Sam had rolled away from Otto and now lay on his side curled up as if he were in severe pain. His face was twisted and white.

Adria laid the police revolver down and gently tugged Sam onto his back. Dark glasses no longer covered his eyes but they were closed now. The glasses lay shattered on the rough floor. Blood was staining the rough cave floor from a hole in Sam's side. Adria felt weak with horror. Was Sam going to die? Dear God, don't let him die!

Sibyl was now back with rope and she was holding the gun on Otto while Larry was trussing his hands and feet. He finished quickly and turned Otto face down.

"I'm going to the house to call an ambulance," Adria called to Larry. "Take this gun, and do what you can for Sam!" Then she was out the entrance and skidding down the embankment to the trail without waiting for an answer.

Adria was only half way up the trail when she met Fritz coming on the run. In one hand he held the deer rifle. "We heard gun shots fired," Fritz said, panting up to Adria, "What's happened?"

"Sam's been shot and Larry has tied up the gunman," Adria said quickly. "Maybe you can help Sam. I'm going to call an ambulance."

She was skidding on down the trail and Fritz' answer followed her, "Sarah was calling the sheriff's office when I left."

Sarah, pale and shaken, met her at the back door. Adria pushed her gently aside and sprinted to the telephone. "A man's been shot," she explained to Sarah as she dialed 911.

A minute later, still gasping for breath, she was giving directions to a capable dispatcher, who assured her a rescue unit would be on the way in minutes.

Sarah followed her as she ran back toward

the door. She held on to Adria long enough to find out that none of the Graham family was hurt.

"But Sam Tillet is hurt bad," Adria said, her breath was still unsteady from her run down the hill.

"Isn't he the one who shot Kandy?" Sarah asked.

"No, he was a suspect but he isn't anymore," Adria said quickly. "Otto Colman, the real gunman was holding us captive at gun point and Sam charged into him like a mad bull. Otto shot him twice."

"The sheriff will be right out," Sarah said. "When we heard those gun shots, we knew they were from the cave by the way they sounded, and we knew you and Sibyl were up there. So Fritz lit out with the gun and I called the sheriff."

"Stay in the house, in case you need to give further directions and so you can direct the ambulance when it gets here," Adria said as she started out the door.

As she raced back up toward the cave, her mind was filled with dread. Was Sam going to die? Dear God, don't let Sam die. "Please don't let him die!"

Chapter 24

When Adria arrived back at the cave, Fritz was holding Larry's bloody shirt, folded into a flat bandage, to the wound in Sam's side. Sam's shoulder didn't seem to be bleeding very badly so perhaps it wasn't too bad.

Adria knelt down beside Sam. He was so white and still. Was he dead? No, someone had unbuttoned his shirt, and she saw the rise and fall of his chest under the dirt-be-smirched undershirt which clung wetly to his thin frame. She spoke through tight lips, "The rescue unit is on its way."

Suddenly Sam's heavily-lashed eyes opened and Adria almost gasped aloud. She was looking into Giles's eyes! Shock must have registered in her eyes, because a crooked grin appeared on his long thin face and he whispered, "Don't tell me I remind you again of that Giles fellow. I'm beginning to be jealous of that guy."

A spasm of pain seemed to slide over his face then and his pallor deepened. His eyes flickered and then closed. His breathing became rapid and shallow and he shifted restlessly. Adria reached over to touch his hand and found it cold and clammy.

"Is-is he unconscious?" Adria whispered.

"I think so, young lady," Fritz said. "Isn't there a blanket or two around here? I'm afraid he's going into shock."

Adria scurried to the locker and brought back two blankets and two pillows. She covered Sam's thin form with the blankets and Fritz directed her to raise his head with a pillow.

"That's right," he said, when she slid a pillow under his head. "Put the other one under it too. We need his head higher."

Adria's heart was beating wildly as she studied his face in bewilderment. Those eyes were Giles' and the shape of his head was also endearingly familiar, only the features were wrong. There was a mystery here and she meant to find out what it was — if Sam lived.

If Sam lived! Of course he would live! Oh God, please make him live. I don't really know this man but I want to know him!

Suddenly Adria leaned forward and lifted an object suspended from a chain about Sam's neck. She hadn't noticed it before. A tingling started inside her as she examined the ring she held in her fingers.

The ring was gold, much too small for a man's finger. It was a girl's senior class ring, one from Adria's own graduating class. She turned the ring so she could see it more clearly in the light of the nearest lantern. With heart banging in her chest, she found what she was searching for, a deep scratch on one side that a sharp rock had made when she had fallen mountain-climbing once. The ring was Adria's own, given to Giles' to wear when they had become engaged!

For a long moment, she stared at Sam's face. Her heart felt squeezed and she found it hard to breathe. What was going on here? Sam's head, forehead and eyes were Giles'. Even the voice was extremely similar and he whistled like Giles.

But the straight nose, cheekbones and chin were not Giles'! And yet, how had this man gotten her ring that he wore on a chain around his neck just as Giles had?

Adria paced the rough floor, returning again and again to Sam's side to stare at his ashen face. It seemed an eternity before the rescue unit arrived though in reality it was a very short time. The paramedics were efficient and soon had the unconscious Sam ready to transport to the hospital.

Before they finished preparing Sam, the sheriff and two deputies arrived and took sullen Otto Colman into custody. Adria told them she planned to follow the ambulance. "Sam will need someone to call his attorney and perhaps relatives, if the lawyer knows of any."

The sheriff asked her to give a brief account of the happenings in the cave, then she was allowed to leave with the ones who carried Sam down on a litter to the waiting ambulance.

"I'll be at the hospital if you need to talk to me anymore," she said as she was leaving.

Adria followed the ambulance in her car and then followed the gurney and attendants into the emergency entrance at the hospital. She moved up along the side of the gurney as they wheeled him quickly down the hall. Sam looked so still and white. Was he going to live? Her fervent silent prayers followed him as they wheeled him away into a sterile white room and shut the door upon her.

Sudden tears rose in Adria's eyes and a feeling of utter desolation swept over her. Sam seemed so weak and he had lost so much blood. Would she ever see him alive again? Dear God, don't let him die! He saved us all! Please keep him from dying!

Adria called his lawyer who promised to come immediately. When Adria asked if she should call Sam's family, Mason Keeley replied that he didn't think there was any.

Kandy's room was around the corner and down the hall from where they had taken

Sam, and Adria went there next. Kandy greeted her happily and said Gentry had gone for a walk. "I ran him out," Kandy said, her dark eyes twinkling. "He needs some fresh air."

"We've found out who shot you," Adria said.

"Not Sam Tillet?"

"No, Otto Colman."

Kandy's dark eyes widened, "The man who beat me up?"

"The same!"

"I knew I was right," Kandy exclaimed. "Did you find out why he attacked me and tried to kill me?"

Before Adria could begin her explanation, Gentry came in. Then Adria related everything she knew about Otto Colman and his connections with Sibyl and Larry. "I hope Sibyl isn't angry with me," she said, "but it's time everything is out in the open. Besides, you are the one who has suffered the most, Kandy, almost losing your life!"

Kandy took the news of what Sibyl and Larry had done amazingly well. "Sibyl would give her life for either Larry or me," she said. "We'll support her to the last degree now. We're family."

When she was finished, Gentry asked, "Is Sam Tillet going to live, Adria?"

Pain filled Adria's eyes, "I really don't know. They're doing all they can. He was so brave. He had to have known there was little chance that Otto wouldn't shoot him full of holes and yet he charged right into him. And hung onto his gun hand until he almost collapsed."

Adria swallowed hard the tears that threatened in her throat and tried to speak brightly, "Kandy, your Sarge is due a champion's medal too. He attacked on command just like he was trained to do and made Otto release the gun. You should be so proud of him!"

After Adria went away to check on Sam, Kandy spoke sadly, "Gentry, I think Adria has fallen hard for Sam and it doesn't look good for him."

"Let's pray right now for Sam," Gentry said, taking Kandy's slim hand in his. "He certainly deserves a chance at life. He saved three of your family and that madman might have come after you again if he hadn't been stopped."

Three hours later a surgeon came out to the waiting Adria and Keeley and reported Sam was holding his own. "He had lost a lot of blood but rallied really well when we gave him whole blood. The bullet went in high on the left side and a rib deflected it downward. There is quite a bit of damage but he should recover completely. The wound on his shoulder was not too serious but will be sore for a while."

"Thank God!" Adria said. "Can we see him — is he conscious?"

"Groggy but conscious," the doctor said. His kindly eyes held a twinkle as he gazed at Adria for a moment, "Taking into account that the young man kept muttering your name before we got him fully anesthetized, I suppose I might let you see him briefly."

He consented to letting the lawyer go in, too. "But neither of you can stay long."

When Adria and Keeley tiptoed into Sam's room they saw a needle in his arm and his face was drawn and white. As Adria stopped near the bed, his dark eyes opened and again she felt her heart constrict with dismay. The eyes looking into hers were Giles' expressive intelligent eyes!

He lifted a thin, weak hand and she took it in her own. "Thanks for coming. You, too, Keeley." A crooked grin curved his pale lips, "Doesn't look like I'm going to need your services much, after all."

His eyes went back to Adria, "No one else was hurt, were they?"

"No one at all — thanks to you!"

"And Sarge and Larry," Sam said deprecatingly.

"The sheriff has Otto Colman in custody," Keeley said. He laid a hand on Sam's arm and said earnestly, "It sounds like you are a hero." When Sam began to shake his head, the lawyer said teasingly, "Better take advantage of it. It doesn't happen to most of us in a lifetime." After a few more words, he excused himself and went out.

"I had better go too, Sam," Adria said, disengaging her hand from Sam's. "You need your rest."

"Looking at your pretty face is very resting to me," Sam said with a grin.

Adria felt herself blushing and he laughed softly.

A nurse came bustling in then and smilingly shooed Adria from the room.

Sam was heavily sedated for the next two days so Adria only saw his sleeping face when she peeked into his room. But the third day when she went into his room he was awake. The nurse warned her she wasn't to stay over five minutes.

"Hi," he said when she slipped into the room. "I'm finally back in the real world."

"Are you in much pain?" Adria asked.

"A little," he admitted. "And so sore that I can hardly move. Come over here so I can see you better." When she moved over to stand next to his bed, he reached a warm hand to take hers in a quick squeeze.

"Thank God that you weren't killed," Adria said earnestly.

A slight frown appeared on Sam's face, "Thank Sarge and Larry," he said dryly. "They're the ones who came to my aid."

"How do you know God didn't put them where they were so they could come to your aid?" Adria said softly. "And how do you know you weren't released on bail so you could come to our aid?"

Sam's frown deepened so Adria changed the subject abruptly. "All charges against you have been dropped. And Otto has all kinds of charges filed against him, among them attempted murder and assault."

"I know," Sam said. "Keeley was in for a few minutes this morning."

"Sibyl sent the painting that was in the cave back to its owner and is willing to repay all the money she received for her reproductions of the other paintings. However, all the paintings were sold to wealthy people in other countries and Otto said there was no way he was giving out their names. So I doubt they will ever know the paintings weren't what they seemed."

"Are Sibyl and Larry in jail for their part in all this mess?"

"No, Sibyl and Larry told the police everything but so far no legal charges have been filed against them."

"I'm sorry your cousins are in this trouble," Sam said. "They seem like real decent folks."

"I'm sorry too, but since they have never been in trouble before and since they are more than willing to give testimony against Otto should be in their favor. It seems that Otto is part of a crime organization that the FBI has been after for a long time."

"We nabbed a real bad number then?"

"Sure did," Adria said. She hesitated, "Sam, do you feel like some serious talking?"

Sam's crooked grin was teasing, "That sounds ominous — but sure, go ahead and talk."

Sam's intent eyes were on her and she lowered her eyes so she could get her thoughts together without "Giles'" eyes staring at her. She cleared her throat and spoke hesitantly. "You had my ring hanging around your neck on a chain."

She lifted her eyes to his, "I gave that ring to Giles when we were engaged."

Sam's eyes suddenly filled with strong emotion — perhaps even pain — and he dropped them but said nothing.

"Sam, where did you get that ring?"

He still didn't answer or look at her and Adria stepped closer to the bed and said gently, "Sam, I think it is only fair that you give me some answers."

Sam closed his eyes and turned his face away but not before she saw the despair there. She leaned over him and put her hand on his arm and said softly, "Please, Sam. Tell me. Is Giles dead? Was he killed in battle. Did he give you my ring?"

"Yes," Sam's finely sculptured head turned toward her and his eyes burned into hers, "Yes," the voice was bitter, "I guess you could say that Giles is dead — dead and buried!"

Adria's face paled. Drawing up a chair, she sat close beside the bed where she could see into Sam's face. "Would you tell me the truth? Is Giles — really dead?"

Sam closed his eyes and drew in his breath raggedly, "I-I guess you have every right to know." When he opened his eyes they were horror-filled. "I'm not sure I can do this now, though."

"I'll come back when you're stronger," Adria said quickly. She stood up, "I'm sorry, Sam. I don't know what I was thinking of, pressing you when you are so weak and have been through so much. I'll go now. I'm sorry to be so thoughtless."

As Sam reached to take her hand, his eyes were kind and filled with a strange sadness, "You were never thoughtless, Adria dear, never! I'm the thoughtless one. I — I meant to be kind but I've only caused you much pain."

Puzzled, Adria started to question him, but suddenly he turned his head away and with a quick squeeze dropped her hand and murmured, "Please, not today. Come back tomorrow. . . ."

His nurse came in then and Adria bade him a quick goodbye and departed.

Adria slept little that night. When she did sleep, she had nightmares — the old nightmares where Giles was calling her begging for her help and she couldn't reach him. She finally got up at three o'clock and tried to read. When it was not even daylight, she got up quietly, had some hot chocolate and took Sarge for a walk up into a misty cloud on the mountainside.

"My life right now is like I'm walking in a cloud of mist," Adria told Sarge. "And always there is Giles' voice calling me." She stopped and looked down into the intelligent eyes of the handsome German Shepherd. "But now sometimes, it's Sam's voice I hear. I'm not sure I know the difference anyway.

"What is Sam going to tell me?" she mused. Part of her cringed with dread. Is Giles dead? No, the way Sam had said he was dead left doubt about it. But something is very wrong, I know. Could Giles have suffered brain damage — in a battle perhaps. Whatever it was, it is so dreadful that Sam can scarcely talk of it.

"But why does Sam look so much like Giles? Is he a relative — a brother?" She started on up the trail, Sarge on the leash. No, she thought, Giles had told her he had no close relatives.

She and Sarge climbed to the gazebo and sat there until the morning sun burned away the mist. "I hope Sam's words burn away the fog in my mind and bring me light," she told Sarge. "And don't burn me to a crisp in the telling!"

But she was not to find out anything new that day. When she arrived at the hospital, a nurse told Adria that Sam had several weakening nightmares during the night and they had sedated him heavily so he could get some rest. Adria felt like bawling. I did that to him, she thought. I started him to thinking on some devastating memory and now look what it has caused!

For two days, she stayed completely away from his room. In fact, Kandy was going home in the morning and Adria had decided to go home to Albuquerque as soon as Sam talked to her and after Kandy was installed in her room at The Lodge again. Late that afternoon, while she was visiting with Kandy, a nurse came with a message. Sam wanted to see her.

Chapter 25

When Adria, with wildly beating heart, entered Sam's room, she found him sitting up with pillows pushed behind his back. His face was still haggard but he was freshly shaved, his dark hair curling about his ears and neck.

Adria felt slightly weak-kneed when she met his dark, heavily lashed eyes — Giles' eyes. She remembered teasing Giles that girls would die of envy at his long dark eyelashes.

Gravely, Sam asked her to close the door. He seemed all business today and Adria felt a quiver of hurt. Did he blame her for causing his nightmares? She moved over to the chair beside his bed and sat down. "I want to apologize for my thoughtlessness the other day," she said earnestly. "I'm afraid I caused the nightmares the nurse said you had."

His tone was impersonal, even brisk. "Don't worry about it. Those aren't the first I've had over this sorry business." He reached for a glass of water and she noticed his hand trembled when he set it down after taking a drink.

"You don't have to tell me anything if you

aren't up to it," Adria said anxiously.

"I want to come clean about everything," Sam said, without looking at her. Then he lifted his head and his eyes were as solemn as his voice. "I must have your promise, though, that you will never repeat what I'm about to tell you. My life could depend upon it."

"Of course — I promise," Adria said.

Sam locked eyes with her and said softly, "I told you that Giles is dead. He is, legally speaking. Giles died and was buried and Sam Tillet rose from his dust."

For a long moment Sam's eyes held Adria's as she struggled to take in his meaning. "Do you understand what I'm saying," he asked her softly.

"You-you," Adria's voice broke and then she went on, "you mean you are Giles?" Suddenly the room seemed to go into a slow whirl and she closed her eyes tightly as she struggled against the faintness rolling over her. Dimly, she heard Sam asking her anxiously if she was all right, and then he was instructing her to put her head down between her knees.

She obeyed and in a moment was lifting her mortified face to see the roguish light in Sam's eyes, "My, my — that's the first time I ever had a girl swoon over me." The words and teasing light in Sam's eyes were so like the old Giles that it brought tears to her eyes.

"I-I'm sorry, but you sure know how to pitch a girl on her face," Adria said as lightly as she could manage. She drew in a quivering breath, "How can you be Giles? Your features are not his."

"I've had extensive plastic surgery," Sam said.

"But why? To disguise yourself?" Adria asked in astonishment. "Is someone after you?"

"The answer to the first is 'no' and to the second is 'yes'."

"J-just tell me what this is all about," Adria said faintly.

"You know I went to war, only I didn't really go to war, I trained to be a secret agent and was sent to one of the South American countries to gather information. I can't reveal much of my activities but I can say that I was a successful spy, for a while."

"Why would you train to be a spy?" Adria asked. "We were going to be married and — and I needed you!"

Sam reached over and touched her cheek with a long finger, "I know, it was a stupid thing to do, but is youth ever sensible? I had a friend who was training for secret service;

it sounded exciting and my friend said he would make a lot of money. I wanted a lot of money to give you a better life than what a forest ranger could make."

"I wanted you, not an easy life," Adria murmured.

"Yes, I know, but perhaps even the excitement of being a spy got to me too. The thirst to pit myself against real danger, to see what I was made of — it all had a bearing, I'm sure." He grinned, "Besides, I only planned to serve for a short while and then I was going back to take up my chosen profession and marry the most wonderful girl in the world!"

Adria stared at him. "But something went wrong?"

"Everything went wrong!" Sam's face went taut and a shudder quivered over his frame. "A buddy and I were almost caught by a drug lord and his men. We managed to get away but only because a family took us in and hid us."

His voice went bleak and he choked and couldn't go on for a moment. "They had children, two pretty little girls and a fat little brown baby." His voice had dropped so low that she had to bend toward him to hear.

He took two shuddering deep breaths and then went on in a calmer voice, "My buddy and I got away but a few days later we were captured. Our captors knocked us around a little, trying to get information on what we had learned of their activities. They had us in a hut out in the jungle. When we wouldn't talk, they darkened the two windows in the place and showed us a film.

"They told us that if we didn't talk, our fate would be the same as the people in the film. 'You caused this,' the leader told us, as he began to roll the film. They had brutalized and killed the family who had helped us, and photographed it all in lurid detail!"

Sam did not speak for a moment and then he looked into Adria's eyes, "The young couple who took us in did it because they were Christians, they said." His voice turned bitter and caustic, "Where was God when he let them die — let them suffer!"

"W-what happened to them?" Adria heard her voice whisper.

Sam shifted his eyes from hers and said in a strained, anguished voice, "They shot them!"

Adria laid her hand on Sam's arm, "Don't torture yourself like this. You'll be sick. . . ."

But Sam seemed not to hear her. "They knocked the husband around for a few minutes and he tried to tell them he didn't know anything. They were trying to make him tell where we had gone and they didn't even know!" Then his voice again dropped low and anguished. "They took the baby and shot it to death in front of their eyes."

Adria realized he was seeing it all again and tried to take her eyes from his haunted face but could not.

"That fine, wonderful man and woman had to watch while those hoodlums killed their children one by one, first the baby and then the little girls. Then before he was killed the husband saw them execute his wife. At last all were piled in a heap on the floor of the little house where they had sheltered us. I'll never forget the agony twisting their tear-wet faces as they shot their little ones to pieces."

He turned to Adria, tears running down his face, and said harshly, "They died with prayers on their lips — but God didn't save them or their children!"

"The drug people would probably have killed them anyway, since they took you in," Adria said gently.

"Yes, I'm sure they would have and the people knew it too, no doubt."

"I'm so sorry," Adria said gently. "W-what did you do after they showed you the pictures?"

A mirthless chuckle burst from Sam's

twisted lips, as he wiped the tears from his eyes and went on, "I don't recall, but my buddy told me later that I went completely berserk. They hadn't tied us up — there were ten men in the room with us — and he said I tore into them like an outraged mother grizzly. He said I knocked them about like they were toothpicks but there were so many of them that they overcame me and beat me until my face was just a pulp."

"Didn't your buddy try to help you?"

"One of the men held a gun on him while it was going on. I was as limp as a rag before he got a chance to grab a gun from the guard and shot his way out of the place. That night he crept back to see if he could find out what happened to me and he found me dumped out in the jungle.

"They must have thought I was dead and so did he at first. Then he was shocked to find a faint heartbeat. He carried me all night and got me to a doctor."

"How did you survive?"

"I don't know. But much of the first several months I wished I was dead almost every hour of every day. The bones in my face were shattered and one glance in a mirror and I wouldn't look again.

But worst of all were the nightmares and

flashbacks. They had to keep me restrained most of the time because I would see those men creeping up on me, or see the vivid scenes of that family being butchered and I'd run amuck, crazy as a loon, until it passed."

"But why didn't you tell me what you were going through? I loved you!"

"I couldn't," Sam said brusquely. "Not until I knew if I was going to be well — and not look like something out of a horror movie." A shudder ran through him and then he resumed. "After a few months, I began to get myself back together again. The government paid for some plastic surgery but when it began to run into an enormous sum, they told me they couldn't afford to pay for any more. I could stay in the hospital but no more expensive plastic surgery was available."

"What did you do?"

"I had decided I would never go back to you looking like a freak, so I spent all the money I had saved — and I think the expensive plastic surgeon must have had mercy on me too. After a number of operations I had a presentable face, though not much like the original."

"But surely you wouldn't think that would matter to me?"

Sam lifted pain-filled eyes to study

Adria's face, "You didn't see me before the surgeries. I wouldn't have wanted your pity."

"Why didn't you come back to me after the surgeries?"

"I couldn't get rid of the flashbacks! I still went berserk several times a week. I even broke the jaw of an orderly. I've had psychologists treat me, taken drugs, had group therapy — I've tried everything! I don't have as many as I used to have but I still have them."

"But won't the memories gradually fade and you will no longer have them?"

"I hoped so and I moved back to New Mexico and checked into the VA hospital in Albuquerque and had more sessions of psychotherapy."

"Why didn't you contact me and tell me what was going on. Perhaps I could have helped you. Besides, I nearly went out of my mind!"

"I'm sorry," Sam said gently, "I did find out where you were working, but that wasn't too good. I couldn't keep away from you. Seeing you again was like fire in my bones and I couldn't get enough of just feasting my eyes on you. I followed you about for weeks before that incident in the old part of Albuquerque, when those guys started to hassle you."

"You were a life saver," Adria said.

"I didn't think you would recognize me but I couldn't be sure, so I always wore dark glasses. I tried to stay away from you but you were like an addictive drug," Sam said. "I was afraid you might notice I was following you but I couldn't seem to quit."

"You should have come to me and explained. I thought you were some weirdo following me!"

"I know that now. I'm sorry."

"Why do you go by the name of Sam Tillet?"

"Oh yes, I forgot to tell you about that." His eyes were grim and bitter. "That was another obstacle. I'm in a protection program. The drug lord has connections in the United States and it was discovered — after they killed my buddy right here in the good old U.S. of A. — that they knew who we were. So the word went out, and records were falsified, that Giles Hughlet was killed in South America by unknown assailants. I was Sam Tillet when I entered the first hospital in the states. I have the rights of a soldier and my record shows I was hurt during a military operation in South America."

"What are you going to do now?" Adria asked.

"I may go back to college — using my veteran's benefits — and get a degree in forestry," Sam said with a crooked grin. "After all, Sam only has a high school education." He chuckled mirthlessly, "I should make straight A's since I already have a degree."

"I'm so sorry, Sam," Adria said. Her eyes brightened, "But you won't be too far away! I couldn't bear it, if I can't see you often."

Sam reached over and took both of Adria's hands in his warm ones, "It won't work," he said gently, his dark eyes tender and pain-filled. "I'm going away when I'm well enough and we must never see each other again. I'm not Giles anymore. I'm Sam Tillet — the veteran who goes berserk and could kill his own wife during one of those blasted spells."

Adria's low cry was almost wild, "No, Sam, you can't do that! I-I'll die if I lose you again!"

But Sam was shaking his head sorrowfully, "I would never do that to you, Adria. I love you too much. Besides the demons that I can't expel, there is the drug family that might find me someday. I could never expose you to danger like I did that priceless family in South America."

Adria tried to not cry, even tried to be angry. After all, hadn't this man caused her enough grief for two lifetimes, she tried to tell herself, but the tears came and she sobbed despairingly.

A nurse stepped in and asked if everything was all right. "I'm all right," Adria said, her voice muffled in the tissues Sam had thrust into her hands. He sent the nurse away.

Sam leaned over and again took both of Adria's hands, "Mason Keeley is taking me to the VA hospital in Albuquerque tomorrow," he said gravely. "I'm strapped for finances so I have to go where I can get free hospitalization until I'm on my feet again."

"I'll go to visit you!"

"No, Adria," Sam was shaking his head, "You mustn't. Remember, Giles is dead. D — E — A — D. You were engaged to him but he's forever gone. You've got to accept that. I should never have come back to New Mexico. It was a mistake. But I kept hoping. . . ." His voice broke on a sob, recovered and went doggedly on, "When I get out of the hospital, I'm going to another part of the country. I may even leave the states, altogether. You must forget me and I must try to do the same."

Adria felt too numb to even cry now and looked at Sam with wide tragic eyes. "Sam," she said, "if you would give your life to Jesus, He could make your mind well."

Hope welled up in her eyes, "Yes, Sam, that is the answer! Jesus could make you well!"

Sam's laugh was coldly cynical and censorious, "I could never serve a god who deserted his followers like he did that Christian couple in South America. No, Adria, I could never be a Christian."

His fine lips curled in a wry grin, "Didn't I read somewhere that Christians should never marry out of their faith. Well — I have none!"

He reached up and lifted the chain, from which dangled Adria's class ring, from his neck. He placed it in her hand and closed her fingers around it. The chain felt warm in her cold hand. Sam's eyes held deep pain but his jaw was set and determined.

She closed her eyes for a moment and drew in a quivering breath. She took her hands out of Sam's and slowly rose to her feet. She felt like she was dying bit by bit, she had to get out of this room!

"I'll pray for you, Sam Tillet," she whispered, as she turned and fled from Sam's presence.

Chapter 26

The next few weeks were the worst time of Adria's entire life because she not only was fighting her grief this time, but for her faith in God, as well. Two years before, when Giles had sent the letter breaking off with her, Adria had still harbored hope that he would come back to her. Now she had no hope. After her talk with Sam, she went back to The Lodge, packed up and went home. Later she could not even recall the explanations she had given Kandy and Sibyl.

Pushing her class ring on its silver chain far back in a drawer out of her sight, Adria cried for hours. But they were not healing tears, but tears of utter despair and desolation. Sam was never coming back. She would never see him again. Strange that her heart had seemed to know that Sam was Giles. She had found Giles — in Sam — and lost him again!

In desperation, she even considered going to the VA hospital and begging Sam to reconsider sharing his life with her but recalling his decisive words she knew it would only prolong her agony, and his. Sam had made a clean break and he wasn't coming back.

"I can't bear it," she sobbed out to God. Then she was angry, furiously so, with God. Maybe Sam was right! God had not delivered that poor couple in South America from death and he had not delivered her either, from the same as death. "I'd be glad to die too, God," she raged. "Them you let die, but me you won't let die!"

Kandy called her and tried to find out what was wrong and even threatened to go to Albuquerque in her weakened condition if she didn't tell her. "You looked like the whole world had caved in when you came into my hospital room and said you were going back to Albuquerque," Kandy said. "Please tell me the problem. Did you and Sam have a falling out?"

"We never had a falling in," Adria said bitterly.

"You fell for the guy. I know you did," Kandy said adamantly. "But if Sam isn't the problem, Adria, you must tell what is troubling you. How can I help, if you won't tell me!"

"I can't tell you anything except that, yes, I did fall for Sam but it just didn't work out. Sam's gone and he isn't coming back," Adria admitted and that was all she would say.

"I'm so sorry," Kandy said, "I'll come

down if that will help."

"You mustn't, Kandy," Adria said, "You are far too weak. I'll get over this too." But she didn't.

She didn't go back to work immediately as she couldn't sleep or eat. She grew thin and her nerves were stretched taut as a violin string. She walked the streets and the malls, and tried to make herself interested in life again — but it was no use.

For her faith in God was also shattered. She couldn't talk to God anymore. When she forced herself to pray, she was soon ranting at God and blaming him for everything. Gone were the restful talks with Jesus. Did God really love her? Or anybody? She would cry herself to sleep then but would be awake in a short while, nerves twanging with remorse and begging God for forgiveness. But almost immediately her thoughts would turn to Sam and she was angry again at God.

Some of the time she also raged at Sam. Why did he give her no choice in this matter? It was her life too! If she chose to share in danger with him, why would he not give her that choice?

"I would go to the ends of the earth with you, Sam," she had sobbed.

But that too, was as empty as raging at

God — and just as fruitless.

She returned to work and found it difficult to write the simplest story. Nothing seemed worthwhile and she saw her boss, and several of the staff, watching her with troubled faces. Her boss even suggested she see a doctor, or take off a few more days of work. Thanking him numbly, she did.

She went to church once but found herself unable to concentrate on the sermon. The people were friendly as usual but she quailed before their solicitous questions. Questions she could not answer. So she left in the middle of the sermon. The pastor called and she gave evasive answers to his kind inquiries and was glad when he hung up. A friend from church came to see her and she didn't go to the door.

What would her Christian friends think if she told them she was no longer on speaking terms with God?

One day, three weeks after she had returned home, Adria rode to the top of Sandia Peak on the tram. Suddenly she found herself seriously contemplating jumping off a high cliff. There would be no more pain something seemed to urge inside her. You could finally rest. No more tormented mind. No more unanswered questions. Peace, that illusive much desired state, would come at last, that persistent whisper seemed to say.

Suddenly the awfulness of what she was considering burst upon Adria. Horror gripping her, she backed away from the edge and ran. "I'm becoming suicidal," she thought, fear now nipping at her heels.

She ran until she could run no more and fell gasping for breath. She lay for a long while where she had fallen.

She lay on a bed of fragrant pine needles under a giant tree. Above her in every direction were the swaying tops of pungent scented pine and fir trees. Silence, like a cathedral was all about her and for the first time in three weeks, Adria could think rationally. Lying on her back, she felt as if she were cradled in the giant arms of green boughs.

She closed her eyes and slept peacefully for the first time in weeks. She awoke several hours later and sat up. The air was warm and smelled sweet and clean. She felt refreshed and suddenly hungry. Clutching at a boulder under the sheltering tree, she climbed to her feet.

She looked up-up-up to the dizzying top of the magnificent tree. The top-most branches swayed gently in the breeze. It has stood here for many, many years, she thought, always reaching up toward God. Cruel frosts, chilling snow, icy storms, heat, winds and drought have thrown themselves against it but it just kept standing here, reaching up to God.

Tears ran down her face but she was scarcely aware of them. "Dear God, how could I ever have doubted your love? The storms must come or we would never grow strong. Trials build character and although you don't keep the trials away, we can be confident that you will be there with us always. Your son gave his life so we could have life — eternal life — with you. You gave your son for us, so you must love us, unworthy though we are."

Under the towering cathedral-like canopy, she bowed her head and said softly, "Please, dear heavenly Father, forgive me for my unbelief."

She even admitted to herself then that she, as a Christian, should not marry a non-Christian. And Sam was most certainly not a Christian!

She was so ravenously hungry that she ate at the snack shack before going back down on the tram and then again when she arrived home. And she called her boss that she would be back to work on Monday. The next day was Sunday and she planned to attend the house of God.

Now it was three months since she had last seen Sam. The deep hurt of losing Sam — Giles, really — was still there but it was bearable now. She had God and caring friends to help her. There were tears sometimes, sometimes even brief depression and despair, but there was also laughter. In time, perhaps, she might find someone else to love. God grant that she could!

She was on her way to The Lodge. Benjamin Graham, her uncle, had died quietly in his sleep last night. The funeral would be tomorrow. Sibyl had called her.

"And I'm sure that Father came to Christ before he died," Sibyl had said. "Ever since I gave my life to the Lord, I have talked to Father daily about God and read the scriptures to him. A few days ago, I asked him if he would like to say a sinner's prayer that he should squeeze my hand, and he did. He even made those sounds as if he is struggling to speak as I prayed. Since then his eyes have held a peaceful look and he died with a smile on his poor twisted lips."

This was a different Sibyl than Adria knew. She had called Adria recently and told her she had gone with Kandy to church and given her life to God. Her near brush with death had decided her.

Larry is still going his own merry way, Adria thought as she drove, but prayer could change all that. There were three praying for him now.

She smiled as she turned the car off the highway onto the gravel road that led to The Lodge. God had been good to Sibyl and Larry. They had told everything to the police and had both been given suspended five year sentences, if they would agree to tell what they knew about Otto and the money laundering in court. Their testimonies would be used to help break up a crime organization who dealt in drugs, prostitution and many other crimes as well.

Sibyl was now painting under her own name. Larry had sold several of her paintings in the past in his gift shop but she had used Katrina Stone instead of her own name. Sibyl had known her father thought painting was frivolous so she had hidden the efforts of her talent from him.

Kandy had told Adria, "Do you know that Gentry and I were admiring a painting in Larry's shop the first day that Gentry and I went sightseeing and didn't know it was hers? Gentry remarked that the child had my face and he was right. Sibyl had used a childhood picture of me as a model for it!"

Adria was swinging into the drive now.

She saw that Gentry's car was already here. He and Kandy had set their wedding date for early fall. Kandy planned to use autumn colors. It should be beautiful, Adria thought.

The family welcomed her and during lunch Sibyl told the family that just that morning an art gallery had called and wanted to show her paintings. "My very own show!" she said excitedly.

Later in the afternoon, while Sibyl was resting and Gentry and Kandy had wandered off together, Adria took Sarge and went up into the forest.

Clouds were hanging heavy over the mountains and it looked like rain might begin to fall soon, but Adria knew they could always take shelter in the cave. Mist began to swirl about them as they neared the cave entrance. "I'm glad I kept you on leash," she told Sarge. "It's getting as dark as the inside of a whale's belly."

She took another step and Sarge suddenly whined. His eyes were staring ahead into the mist and his tail began to wag. She took a firm hold on the lead as he whined again and strained against the leash. Fear lanced through Adria. Who was out there? Suddenly from the swirling mist the warbling of bird-calls began.

Adria thought her heart would leap from her body and her hands on the leash were suddenly icy cold. As she stood trembling in the trail, the bird-calls changed to a whistled rendition of "I Dream of Jeannie."

"Am I losing my senses," she gasped aloud.

A dark figure, indistinct in the mist, rose from the large boulder just below the cave entrance and a low husky voice began to sing her song.

It was Sam's voice!

Chapter 27

Sam thought he had given Adria up long ago but his anguish had been just as keen and unbearable as when he sent Adria away before. But he had the consolation that he had done the only thing possible for them both.

And he was sure he had been right the first afternoon after he was back at the VA hospital in Albuquerque. A doctor and several student-doctors had crowded around his bed. When a couple of the students reached in their white-coat pockets for pens, his overwrought mind had thought they were after weapons. His mind had suddenly flipped out and he had gone "ape".

It had taken several men to subdue and sedate him.

He was weak and sick afterward and his wounds were damaged. But worse were his feelings of utter hopelessness and fear that he might hurt someone badly — or kill someone.

Through the long, nightmare-haunted night that followed, he wished he had died when he was so near death in the jungles. It would have been so much better for everyone, he thought.

After his stitches had been repaired, the doctors kept him sedated for several days. "I guess they'll make a drug addict out of me now," he had muttered to himself. But actually he was relieved. If he was asleep or drowsy, at least he was harmless.

Two weeks of psychotherapy followed. He didn't have another "spell" but the fear of one was always there to haunt him.

The agony of losing Adria had lessened a little by now and he tried to make some plans for his future. Wryly, he wondered if he had one. He came up with several ideas and discarded them all. College was out for now. His nerves were still very unstable and the strain of exhaustive study might flip him over the brink and during one of those eerie attacks, he might hurt someone.

One of his doctors suggested he might want to consider work in the open, perhaps herding sheep in the back country away from people. "Something like that is what I may have to do," Sam agreed. "My greatest fear is hurting someone."

But he liked people and he wondered if the loneliness would drive him out of his mind. If only I could return to forestry, he thought. He had studied botany and biology and knew much about wildlife, and he loved working with animals in their wilderness habitats.

He began to consider school again. Perhaps he could try a semester, at least. There hadn't been any more "spells". Maybe he was free of them, he hoped fervently. Because of the crowded condition in the hospital, he had now been moved into a ward with a number of other patients. He enjoyed their company and was quickly a favorite because of his quick wit and concern for the other men's problems.

He had left his bed one morning and was standing near the center of the room talking with another patient when a new patient, not knowing Sam's condition, came up behind him and playfully locked one arm around his neck. In a flash Sam flipped him over his head and the man landed on a bed nearby. It was unoccupied at the moment, Sam saw thankfully, but the man rolled and fell off on the other side. White-faced, the man picked himself up and ran out of the room.

The room had gone as silent as a tomb. Every eye was glued on him like he was a monster of some kind, faces incredulous and fearful. Muttering he was sorry, Sam stumbled from the room ashamed and despairing. Fortunately the patient he hurtled over his head wasn't really hurt. That day Sam was moved back to a private room.

It was one of the lowest points of his life since he had come back to the States. Because he knew something the doctors didn't. When he flipped that man over his head, he had not been having a "spell". It had been an automatic reflex — training. I'm trained to be a fighter, he had thought in despair, not to live in the world of normal people.

What am I going to do, he thought desperately throughout that sleepless night. I no longer fit anywhere. I should be away from people — for their safety — he thought bitterly, and yet I would die of loneliness. I need people. I like people. And yet this scourge, this demon inside me, will not let me co-exist with people.

A male nurse looked in on him and he pretended sleep. They were much too free with tranquilizers and sleeping pills here. He certainly didn't want to become a dope head. He had enough problems already!

His mind drifted to Adria. Dear, sweet Adria — if only there was a way he could be with her! Have her for his wife! Fierce longing rose in him so strong that he groaned aloud, then stifled it in a pillow. The thought of Adria had been the only thing that had kept him sane those first nightmarish months in the hospital after he had been nearly beaten to death. Until he had seen his face!

He smiled grimly into the dim room, "I even overcame that obstacle with a new face. But I didn't know then that I would have these devilish 'spells'! If only there was a way to conquer them! If only. . . ."

Tears of frustration and longing welled into his eyes. Adria! He had loved her from the first time he ever saw her. It had been a marvel to him that she loved him too. Still loved him, even after he had dumped her!

But he could never subject her to the terror and danger of one of his "spells". He grimaced. If he didn't hurt her himself, there was always the danger that the vengeful drug lord would find him and exact his revenge.

"If only there were a way," he said for perhaps the hundredth time since he came back to Albuquerque.

Suddenly — like a whisper of cool breeze, he heard Adria's voice: "If you would give your heart to Jesus, he could make you well."

He seemed to feel the pressure of her hand as the voice rippled through his mind again, soft and insistent, "If you would give your heart to Jesus, he could make you well."

Sam sat up in bed and shook his head savagely. He knew better than that! Dear Adria had been deceived. God — if there were such a thing — did not love his creation. He seemed to take pleasure in their suffering. That was not love! So it was idiotic, and pure fantasy, for Adria to believe that God would desire to heal anyone, especially someone like himself who had all but cursed Him!

Sam tried to relax. The night was wearing on and he hadn't been to sleep once. Well, he consoled himself, maybe I'll sleep all day and not be a menace to anyone!

He thought back to his days before he had gone into the secret service. Carefree and happy, he and Adria had thought there was nothing that could ever come between them and happiness together. Till death do us part! There were worse things than death!

Adria! His mind caressed her name. He tried to recall just how she had looked when he saw her last and then drew back from the vivid recollections. Adria, crying wildly when she knew they could not be together!

His eyes filled with helpless tears. What grief he had caused her when all he wanted was to bring her happiness and joy!

He summoned her face to his memory and then he saw her as she had stood, still and ashen before him, just before she ran out of the room. Her voice rang in his memory, brittle with grief and unshed tears, "I'm going to pray for you, Sam Tillet!"

And I imagine she has, probably every day! Not that it will do any good!

Or would it? The astounding thought seemed to come from somewhere outside of his own mind.

Brutally he expelled the thought from his mind. Of course it wouldn't do any good! Why would God care what happened to Sam Tillet? He hadn't seemed to care what happened to that brave couple in South America. He had let them be shot down in cold blood — and let them see their children butchered as well.

But what if prayer did help? The thought seemed to shoulder its way into his consciousness without his permission. And it did not go away, although he tried to scoff it into oblivion. It clung on the edges of his mind with the persistence of a Texas cockle burr. He tried to think of other things but the thought was there, waiting for his answer.

Finally he let the thought remain and examined it, tried to at any rate. He had never tried prayer, he reasoned. Could there be something to it? But that couple — he now recalled that he hadn't even known their names — who hid him and his buddy, they had been praying people. In that horrible film he had heard them praying as their children were being put to death. They had said something like, "Be with us, Jesus."

But what if — yes, what if there were something to this prayer business. Christians put great store in it. A daring thought presented itself. What if he tried it? Wasn't that the only way he would ever know if God was really out there somewhere — if this Jesus that Adria talked about so fondly, was real?

But how did one go about praying, he wondered. He had never prayed in his life. The uncle who had raised him was not a church-goer and scorned those who were. He pondered upon it. Somewhere he had heard someone say that prayer was just talking to God. Well, if that were so, it shouldn't be too hard.

Opening his eyes, he looked through the half open door. That male nurse mustn't see him trying this. He would be convinced Sam Tillet had flipped out of his skull! Sam's room was at the end, and down the hall he could see two female nurses chatting together, and the male one was sitting in a chair, tipped back against the wall reading a magazine. Sam looked at his watch. It was 3:00 in the morning.

He closed his eyes and feeling utterly ridiculous, he spoke softly, "God, if you are really up there, please hear and answer this prayer. I don't know if you are real or not but if you are, I apologize for speaking against you. Adria is sure you love people but I'm not so sure you do. But if you do, and are hearing me, let me know you are real."

He opened his eyes to see if anyone was coming. No one was. He closed his eyes and continued. It was getting easier, he realized.

"Jesus, if you are real, I want to ask a favor. Heal my mind and make it well again. Take away the torment that's in there. And God, while you are about it, would you make me understand why that couple and their children had to die when they loved and served you?

"I guess that's about all, Jesus. I really hope you are up there, and really do love guys like me because it would be a great comfort to me to know you care. Amen!"

Sam was relieved to have it over with. He was giving this prayer thing a good chance and that's all anyone could do. Strangely he now felt calm and relaxed. He quickly fell into a deep sleep and did not dream once during the remainder of the night.

He didn't wake up until the breakfast trays came the next morning at eight. All through the meal and for much of the morning, he waited expectantly. He didn't know what he was waiting for but — well, hadn't he prayed? If God was going to answer, he was ready.

By noon, when nothing unusual had happened, he began to experience disappointment, even bitterness began to rise. I should have known it wouldn't work, he thought. By afternoon, deep disappointment set in and depression tried to grip him.

At three, the chaplain came into his room. "Thought you might need something to read," he said. He laid a Bible on the side of his bed and after exchanging a few desultory words, he left. For a few minutes Sam continued trying to interest himself in a sports article he was trying to read. He realized then that he also had been trying to ignore the Bible laying on his bed.

"Just what I need," he muttered, "a book about God who doesn't even answer prayer."

After staring at it a few minutes, he picked it up and thumbed through a few pages. At least this one was in modern English — a New King James version, it said on the front. The few times he had picked one up before, the words had been some kind of hard to read English.

Suddenly he thought, Oh, well, I might as well give this a try too. If I try both prayer and Bible reading, and they both don't work, I can tell those religious fanatics a thing or two! And I'll keep an open mind, he thought virtuously.

He found Genesis a little unbelievable at first, but he reminded himself that he was going at this with an open mind. But after a while he began to get into the stories of the men and women and he was reading with real enjoyment. By dinnertime he had finished Genesis.

All through his meal he read, and then until the nurse made him turn out his light. And he pursued it again the next day.

He decided the author of Proverbs had a good head on him and some of the Psalms were written by guys just like him, who seemed to not always understand things but were searching for answers.

In First Kings 17, he found a man he liked, Elijah, the Tishbite. He was a man's man — even had the king shaking in his boots! That fiery prophet challenged the queen's own four hundred prophets to a dual between his god and theirs. But at the end of the story, when God had even answered by fire and had proven to the people that God was really God, Elijah ran like a scared rabbit from the queen. A bit disappointing.

Then he read something that seemed to hit him a wallop under the ribs. When Elijah was so discouraged that he prayed to die, God sent an angel two nights in a row with food for Elijah, with the words, "Arise and eat, because the journey is too great for you."

That's my problem, he thought. The journey is too great for me. God had cared for Elijah. He actually sent an angel to feed him, and Elijah took a journey of forty days on that food! He liked that thought: angel food. Perhaps, he thought whimsically, I need some angel food!

Sam read the rest of the day and found himself reluctant to go to bed. He was amazed at himself! This was weird — Sam Tillet reading the Bible and liking it! What was getting into him?

The rest of that week, Sam pored over the pages of the Bible. He read all of some books and portions of others, but some things began to make sense as he read and then pondered on what he read.

The people in the Bible were not super heroes. They were people just like himself, with faults and questions, even unbelief sometimes. Some real men of God even had sinned and had to repent!

But one thing quickly became apparent to him, God did care for those who served and loved Him. Many of them he delivered and even made some rich — strangely others he let die, like the couple in South America. In The Acts of the Apostles, many people gave their lives for their faith. But now he knew how they could, for he had found a promise Jesus made to them before he himself was crucified, "Lo, I am with you always."

Sam had always shrunk away from recalling the film of his friends who had given their lives because they helped him and his buddy. But now he pushed the horror from his thoughts and summoned the grisly scenes to his mind. Heart beating madly, he forced himself to recall the scene just before the man and woman died. What they had said before they died had never been important to him. Now it was.

Willing his cowering mind to recall the scene, he could see their faces, hear their voices. First he heard them say clearly, "Jesus be with us."

Before, his mind had not dwelled on anything but the carnage and cruelty, but now he allowed his mind to recall the faces of his friends. Although there were tears on both faces, there was no bitterness. After the wife was dragged from her husband's side and executed, Sam saw them throw the man over the bloody bodies of his beloved family and he also was riddled with bullets.

Sam dwelled on the face of that man which the camera had brought up close to the viewers of the film. That face had always puzzled him. A slight smile was there and the lips had uttered strange words, "Thank you, Jesus, for being with us."

Now Sam understood! Jesus had been with them even through their awful deaths!

There were some things that no one perhaps could explain, like why God delivered some and let others die. But, live or die, Jesus never forsook them. Never! He was with them!

And where were they now? From his reading, he knew the answer to that one too! His tension eased and he let his breath out in an audible sigh. In his mind, he could almost see them standing well and strong in a marvelous place where there would be no more death — or suffering. They were safe!

His friends were safe! And very happy!

Later that day he found a scripture in Psalm 116:15 that all but took his breath away: "Precious in the sight of the Lord is the death of his saints."

We always think of death as something horrible, he thought, while in reality, for the Christian it is the father just calling his children home to the wonderful place he has prepared for them! A glorious homecoming!

Tears wet his cheeks. If they could see him, his martyred South America friends were probably pitying him! They were at peace and he was still here struggling with his problems.

He realized suddenly that a nurse was standing by the bed. "Is there something wrong?" she asked in a worried tone.

He laughed softly, "No, not a thing is wrong!"

She looked puzzled and when he said no more she went out, probably to tell the other nurses they had better watch him closely! He chuckled. But he felt good! Real good!

He felt like jumping out of bed and running up and down the halls for joy. Wouldn't the nurses and doctors know he had flipped his lid for good then!

Because he realized now, the words out of

the Bible had banished the horror from that memory that had haunted his dreams and waking hours for so long. Now he knew why people of God could give their lives for their beliefs: Death held no terror when Jesus was walking with them. What was life anyway? Only a shadow, in light of what God had prepared for their eternal life. Absent from the earth, present with Jesus!

I feel remade, he thought, and then chuckled. "I believe that's what the Bible meant when it said, 'You must be born again!' "

He humbly bowed his head and in a few simple words asked Jesus to come into his life, forgive him for past sins, and teach him to walk in God's ways.

Chapter 28

Adria stared into the swirling mist as Sam began to walk toward her. She was trembling and put her hand on Sarge's head to steady herself. It couldn't be Sam — and yet it was! Mentally, she tried to put a calming hand on her galloping heart, but it leaped to meet the apparition moving toward her.

Sam stopped a few steps away and stood looking at her. Adria unsnapped Sarge's leash and he rushed to Sam. He laid long slim fingers on the dog's head but continued to gaze at Adria. His dark eyes seemed to hold a glow she had never seen there before. Then he spoke softly, "I heard about your uncle. I'm very sorry."

Disappointment tore at her heart. Sam had only come back to offer condolences on her uncle's death! You would have no right to marry him anyway, her mind scolded her, even if he had come to see you. He isn't a Christian.

She tried to speak calmly, "Thank you. It was kind of you to come. Are you going to the funeral?"

"I'd like to," Sam said. "In fact, I'd like to go with you, if you don't mind."

"Certainly," she said numbly. But her heart was crying, Why did you come back? I was doing fine until I saw you again. Why do you torment me, Sam Tillet!

Ignored, Sarge went gliding away to pursue his own interests. Sam continued to stare at her intently without speaking.

Feeling her face growing hot, Adria said the first thing that popped in her mind, "You're looking well, Sam."

And he was. His lean form had filled out so he no longer had a gaunt look.

His lips curved into a crooked grin, "I should be, I've been eating angel food."

Her heart missed a beat. What an odd thing to say. Had Sam's mind slipped a cog?

He moved closer to her until he was looking down into her eyes, "I never get tired of looking at you, Adria Graham."

"I-I thought you had gone away for good." Adria heard herself stammering.

"I hadn't planned to ever come back," Sam said, "but someone by the name of Adria must have been carrying out her threat of praying for me. I decided to try prayer myself, and then when God didn't seem to answer my prayer to make himself real to me, I decided to go whole hog and read the Bible too."

Adria felt her knees go weak. What was

Sam saying? "You don't mean you — you . . . ?"

Sam's chuckle was tender. "Yes, I mean God answered prayer after all. He sent me a Bible by the hands of the chaplain and the words of that marvelous, powerful book did the rest. I call it angel food. You know, from the story of Elijah, when an angel fed him when things really got rough for him. I became a born again believer better than two months ago."

Tears filled Adria's eyes and she tried to wipe them away but felt strong gentle hands doing it for her. She looked up into Sam's face and saw such love and tenderness there that she felt her heart melting like butter in a microwave oven.

Then those "Giles' " eyes were looking deep into hers. He drew a small jewelry box from his sweater pocket and took out a ring. "I believe this belongs to you," he said softly.

His eyes were questioning as he took her left hand. "May I place this on your finger, Adria Graham? This time for ever and ever."

She stretched out her fingers and said a little breathlessly, "You may, Sam Tillet."

Dream of dreams! Sam was now holding her close to his rapidly beating heart and then his warm lips covered hers.

Much later, they sat with clasped hands on the rock below the entrance to the cave in the crisp morning air.

"I'm free of those 'spells,' " Sam said. He laughed cryptically. "I had a chance recently to put it to the test. I was fool enough to be strolling in a park in Albuquerque one night and several young hoodlums came at me with knives, demanding money. I didn't freak-out at all, but I did give them the scare of their lives. And I was as lucid and cool as the air up here is right now."

He chuckled again, "I told my therapist about accepting the Lord as Savior and he looked a little embarrassed but said he had read that prayer was good therapy.

"Are you still going to live under the name of Sam Tillet?" Adria asked.

A thoughtful look came into Sam's eyes, "I could go back to being Giles now. I called the man I took orders from, to thank him for putting up my bail money and to tell him I was no longer a suspect in Kandy's shooting. He said a rival drug organization had wiped out the drug lord that was after me and I'm free of danger."

He turned to Adria, "What do you think? Would you be more comfortable with Mrs. Giles Hughlet than Mrs. Sam Tillet."

"I don't care what name you use, I just want the man," Adria said with a laugh. Her voice became serious, "But you wouldn't have to repeat college again if you went back to being Giles."

"My director said he would fix it up with the college if I wanted to continue on as Sam."

He looked deep in Adria's eyes, "I don't think I'm Giles anymore." He grinned impishly, "Except I stole his girl."

"Are you still going into forestry work?"

"It's what I love," Sam said eagerly, "and I've already applied for a job as a forest ranger and I'm quite sure I'll get it as soon as the college papers are taken care of.

"I've finished my book and sent it to a publisher. I might be interested in doing some more writing on wildlife, after I get established in a job.

"Now," he said, taking both of Adria's hands in his and kissing each in turn, "When are you going to become Mrs. Sam Tillet?"

At that moment Sarge came charging back from his exploring, and went barking past them down the path. Startled, Adria looked up and saw Kandy and Gentry coming up the path together.

She slid off the rock, and Sam rose to

stand behind her, his arms encircling her waist. Adria saw Kandy's eyes widen with shock as she took in the intimate scene.

"We were getting worried about you," Kandy said.

Adria spoke from the comforting circle of Sam's arms, "I want you two to meet my fiancé Sam Tillet." To Sam, she said, "This is my cousin Kandy and her fiancé Gentry."

Before Kandy and Gentry could recover from their surprise, Adria tilted her head to look into Sam's face, "Would you mind if we made it a double wedding?"